His Secretive Lover

Elizabeth Lennox

CONTENTS

Chapter 1

The dark figure stopped in her tracks, listening carefully, not even allowing herself to breathe. The silence was thick, but something was wrong. The carpeting had suppressed her steps, but she knew that, in the night, every sound, every moment was louder than during the daytime hours.

She closed her eyes and relaxed her mind, letting all the sounds become louder and the movements almost a physical vibration. Relaxing helped her focus all her other senses, her mind working hard to grasp if there was a real threat or if she'd just imagined something. She'd been trained from childhood and knew what to do, how to react and had contingency plans in place. Her training had been thorough.

Total silence. She kept her eyes closed, her body still. Listening.

There it was, she thought with a cheeky, secret smile, her body still frozen in place. The shuffling sound was barely there, but someone was trying to creep up on her.

She would have laughed with delight, but she knew that would give her presence as well as her location away. Silence was the most important aspect of this night. Without silence, she would be caught.

With stealth built up over years of practice, she grabbed the last object in the middle of the desk, then climbed the rope right back up into the ceiling. She suppressed an inner giggle and watched through the air conditioning vent as the large, awkward figure moved into the office. Overhead lights were turned on and the dark head moved to the right and left. As much as she'd like to watch, she knew better than to remain still at this point in the mission. She slowly turned, her body slithering down through the vents. She didn't wait around to see if the inept, power-hungry security guard would spot her through the metal slats.

Gliding lithely through the air system, she made her way back to her starting point. At the last moment, she hesitated, feeling the hairs on the back of her neck rise up. Those little hairs had saved her neck on more than one occasion so she'd learned to listen to their silent warning.

Pausing, she lifted herself higher, using all her upper body strength to pull up another three inches. With that, she knew she was basically invisible to the cameras that she'd already put on a loop. But her position also meant she was invisible to anyone coming out the door directly beneath her. If she hadn't done all those workouts recently, she never would have made it to this point before the guard burst through the door for his nightly, if off schedule and unsanctioned, cigarette and whiskey break.

In that moment, her heart rate accelerated to triple time and she felt a renewed shot of adrenaline spike through her body. She bit her lip and looked around, trying to determine if her back-up escape plan was still viable. She saw the door and the window above it and knew she could do it.

With grim determination, she lifted herself higher up, swung her leg over the ledge and looked down. It was higher than she was used to, but a glance behind her showed that she couldn't go back the other way. With a grin, she sprang forward and caught the opposite ledge just in time. Her gloved hands gripped the edge with just enough strength to pull herself forward once again. With a grunt, she swung her body left, then right, then left again, gaining enough momentum and, at the last moment, swung her whole body over the ledge. With that, she was home free. She got to her feet, maintaining a crouch as she sprinted across the rooftop. The ladder was in sight and she scanned the area. Sure enough, the guards were still focused on the opposite side of the building.

She pulled the harness over her head, then strapped it around her waist and thighs. This was the good part, she thought with relish. Hmmm…maybe the theft part was the best. Or perhaps it was the planning. She really loved planning things out, figuring out all the details. Or maybe, the best part was when she slipped by the guards without them even knowing something had happened.

She smiled in remembrance of the job and the incomparable excitement. It was all good, she thought as she snapped the last of the hooks into place and tightened the harness. With careful eyes, she checked all of her equipment one last time. This was not the time to be careless. She'd already gone over everything four times, but this equipment check would be just as important as the first.

Once she was confident that everything was in place and all the connectors were secure, she moved over to the side of the building, taking a moment to look out over the fabulous city. Chicago really was a beautiful town. Thankfully, she hadn't planned this adventure during the winter months but even now as the October wind blew over the lake and through all the tall buildings there was a definite bite to the air. It was getting colder. This might be the last time she could take this route until springtime, she thought with regret.

With a shrug of her shoulders and an eager smile on her face, she took one more breath, grasped the rope, and threw herself over the ledge with barely a sound.

Down she went! With a whoosh, she flew down the side of the building. She dropped fifty stories down in just seconds, feeling the cold air swish around her. When she was about two thirds of the way down, she clamped the brake that slowed her fall. She was only three inches from the ground before she came to a full and silent stop. It took two more snaps and her thumb flicked the release. The rope zipped up into its carrier, the carrier was stuffed into her leather bag and the harness was stashed into a pocket. Only fifteen seconds after placing her feet on the sidewalk, there was no evidence that she had been here.

She stuffed everything into her bag, turned her hoodie inside out so the pink part was showing instead of the black and slung her bag over her shoulder. She'd done it, she thought with increasing excitement. Maybe this was the best part. Walking away, feeling the thrill of success and the adrenaline pumping through her system. She'd gotten into the office, accomplished her goal and gotten out of the building without anyone knowing she'd even been there.

She almost skipped down the sidewalk but she suppressed the urge, knowing she was supposed to be inconspicuous.

CHAPTER 2

Ryker smiled inwardly as he pulled into his parking spot, but not a hint of that personal satisfaction showed on his handsome features. Ryker was known to be reserved, cool and in control. He rarely put his emotions on display unless he was alone with his brothers. And even then, he was the eldest, needing to be the calming influence. He knew his responsibilities and took them very seriously.

That didn't mean he couldn't appreciate life, he thought as his eyes looked around for the woman.

To the casual observer, he knew that he generally looked serious and intent, but he didn't really care. The opinions of others were of no consequence; he had more important things to worry about than whether someone perceived him as likable. Ryker didn't mind that his staff was intimidated by him. It enabled him to run The Thorpe Group more effectively. He not only had his entire division to run, he was also responsible for the whole company not to mention his three younger brothers who tended to lean towards the boisterous side of life. Thankfully, they didn't fight as much as they used to.

Well, Xander did, but that was because of…Ryker sighed as he thought about that situation. Xander was the second oldest and in charge of the family law division of The Thorpe Group. Ryker thought about the cynicism he'd seen recently in his younger brother. It wasn't healthy, and Xander was definitely becoming more jaded. Maybe that's why the arguments between he and their office manager, Autumn, were getting more…pointed.

Stepping out of his black Tesla sedan, he lifted his briefcase and walked efficiently towards the building's entrance. He timed it perfectly every day and, sure enough, there she was. The exquisite woman with curly blond hair was hurrying into the building on the opposite side of the courtyard. She was lovely and had the sexiest walk, even when she was rushing.

He waited until she was through the doors, watching her for as long as possible before he proceeded into his building. It was a morning ritual that he intended to stop, as soon as he could figure out how to get her to agree to dinner with him. She was painfully shy, he knew. On previous occasions he'd tried to get her attention, but she'd just scurried away after a brief glimpse in his direction.

They played this game every morning, staring at each other across the courtyard, both of them obviously interested but she was too timid and ran away before he could figure out how to interact with her. He'd tried to speak with her once when they ran into each other at the deli. She'd been even more beautiful up close but she'd blushed and hurried out the door, not even getting her lunch in her rush to get away from him. He'd watched her blond curls and extraordinary figure hurry out the door as quickly as her heels could carry her but he'd caught her blush as well as the small gasp that escaped from her lush mouth as soon as she saw him.

A weaker man might be discouraged but not him. That woman was worth the effort, he told himself as he pressed the elevator button for his floor. He would have her sitting across a restaurant table from him very soon. He walked into his office, his assistant, Joan, meeting him at the doorway to the lobby as she did every single morning, following behind him as she read through his early morning messages.

"And lastly, Jason Moran left a message last night, wanting to speak with you urgently. This is his third message in two weeks," she told him without any kind of expression on her face. Joan knew not to be judgmental about any of the issues that came through this office. If her boss hadn't called the man back, there was a reason.

Ryker's eyes slashed over to Joan's. "Jason?" he repeated, his irritation at the man's persistence annoying. "I gave Jason to Martha as a client," he explained, referring to one of the other lawyers in his group. "I know she called him back the last time he called. What does he need to speak with me about?"

Ryker knew that Jason Moran worked in the building across the courtyard. The same building in which his introverted stranger worked. That was a promising development, he thought as he took that message and glanced down at the writing. Perhaps Jason could give him more information about the lovely mystery woman.

Making the decision quickly, he handed the pink square paper back to Joan and continued into his office. "Tell Jason I can see him this afternoon. Give him whatever opening is available on my calendar after my lunch meeting."

Joan nodded and made a note, then turned and walked out of his office to follow his instructions.

CHAPTER 3

Cricket leaned against the back of her office door, breathing deeply of the cool air and trying to slow down her frantic heart rate. She couldn't believe that she felt so exhilarated just because that man watched her walk into the building. Even from a distance, the look was so hot, so intense she felt like she was going to burn up as she walked from the parking garage to the door and then into the building.

Often, on her drive into the office, she tried to talk herself into actually looking at the man, maybe acknowledging him. She'd seen him up close once and he was…amazing! She'd been such a wimp that day. She'd seen his intention to talk to her, to actually communicate, but she'd run away. It was one thing to have a secret infatuation with a man, to build up stories about him and wonder what it would be like to actually talk to him and meet him. She imagined herself sitting down with him in a fancy, elegant restaurant, enjoying witty repartee while he laughed at her quick wit and pithy observations.

Alas, she wasn't quick witted and she rarely had profound reflections about people other than whether they had adequate security or if their jewelry was real or fake. Other than that, her normal, some might say tedious and boring, life revolved around numbers and finding the stories in the numbers. She might be able to sneak into a high security building without being noticed or find variances down to the penny in a multi-million dollar project, but conversing with a gorgeous man? Nope, she was too shy. Especially around her tall, terrifyingly huge and intimidating morning-man.

She really needed to change her schedule so she wasn't showing up at the exact same moment he was arriving each day. But then she smiled inside her tiny office where no one else could see, her body's reaction slowing down. As long as he continued to arrive at the same time, she'd probably keep the same schedule that had her driving up at the same moment. Her mind relished the zing that she got from his look each morning which was better than a double shot of espresso. It might be silly, looking forward to simply seeing a man every morning, but she loved her morning excitement. If she changed her schedule, she'd miss that man terribly.

She should be brave and just talk to the guy. Every morning, she set her alarm clock so her morning was timed to park at the exact right time, skipped breakfast if she was running late, went around the block a few times if she was early…all so she could get a glimpse of him each morning. It was more than a little pathetic, she told herself.

But the idea of actually talking to him, of meeting him face to face instead of across the courtyard set her whole body to shivering in fear. What would she say to him? What could they possibly have in common? He looked like some sort of executive while she was a lowly accountant. She'd probably trip on her own feet if she got any closer to him. He made her so nervous just with a look!

With a sigh, she sat down behind her dull, brown laminate desk and pulled her chair in close, turning on her computer and pulling the large stack of messy and poorly written expense reports closer, forcing her mind away from one dazzling, sexy and scary man. Now that she'd had her morning jolt it was time to start her day. Cricket smiled as she sifted through the stack of papers. She might be a boring, cautious accountant but that didn't mean she wasn't also a secret adrenaline junkie.

Speaking of which, she thought silently…

With an inward giggle, she went back to her office door and opened it once again. She definitely didn't want to miss this morning's excitement. Last night's adventure had been more fun than all the rest because she'd almost gotten caught by that security guard. Well, not almost. She'd been pretty stealthy last night but she'd enjoyed the extra challenge when she'd seen him through the ventilation screen.

And now it was show time. Her boss would walk into his office, see what she'd done and the show would begin. She couldn't wait to hear the outcry when her boss walked into his office.

Last night's escapade was yet another reason she probably shouldn't even think about the elegant stranger. Most likely, he confronted the people who irritated him head on. Cricket had a knack for being creative, but it was a silly, passive aggressive creativity. Her antics might be amusing, but still…she should just get a new job instead of dealing with Jason Moran's petty ways.

She smiled and sat back down at her desk, working diligently at the tiresome expense reports that had been piling up over the past few days, scowling at the mostly handwritten notes and trying to interpret the scribbles. Why couldn't this company automate these reports? She'd submitted a proposal to do just that last month, had even included the cost of a relatively simple software program that would expedite the whole process and help employees get their reimbursement checks more quickly. Unfortunately, she hadn't heard a word from Jason Moran. His silence told her that there was no way he was going to spend any money on something like a basic software package, even if it saved him more money in the long run.

When she finished one expense report and set it up to be processed for payment, she pulled the next one forward, reminding herself that she'd chosen to become an accountant. She could have gotten a degree in any subject but accounting had suited her needs perfectly. And she was pretty good at it too. One had to have the ability to pay attention to small details to get this job done well which meant that the skills her mother and father had taught her growing up were perfectly suited to being an accountant.

So what if she hated every moment of her day? It paid well and gave her the sense of security that she needed. That feeling was more important than loving one's job. She'd hated the insecurity growing up, wishing desperately that her parents hadn't been so good at their chosen profession. So no matter how much she loathed this job, she reveled in that sense of peace.

This job might be mind-numbingly boring and tedious but it kept her out of prison, which is something her parent's occupation couldn't guarantee.

Her mind was focusing on the expense reports but, once she got into a rhythm, she was able to whip through the stack in record time. There were a few that had messy handwriting and nonsensical amounts but most were pretty straightforward. Those were so easy she could almost do them in her sleep.

"Hey Cricket," Debbie, one of the other accountants poked her head into her office. "How about lunch today?" she asked.

Cricket looked up and smiled. "I'd love it," she replied, relieved to have an excuse for a break from entering numbers into spreadsheets and software programs for an hour. But then her eyes turned wary. "What about Mr. Moran?" she asked in almost a whisper.

Debbie's smile brightened and her hand waved away the concern about their boss. "I've already checked with Dorothy," Debbie replied, referring to their boss's assistant, "and he has a lunch scheduled. So there won't be any flak from trying to take a break today."

"Excellent!" Cricket exclaimed, relieved and excited about just getting some fresh air not to mention talking about something that didn't have to do with numbers.

Jason Moran was possibly the worst boss in the world, Cricket thought. But he paid well and provided excellent benefits to his employees, probably because he was such a horrible human being and the salary and perks he provided were the only way he could keep people on staff. Otherwise, Jason Moran walked around the office yelling at people to work harder, stop taking breaks, belittling some of the more junior staff members and just generally being a jerk. Interns rarely lasted more than a week or two because he used their free labor to accomplish the tedious administrative work he was too cheap to pay someone a good salary to do.

The man didn't even like people leaving the office for their lunch breaks. Legally, he couldn't stop employees from taking an hour for lunch, but he made snide comments when he noticed someone actually leaving for their break. He preferred having people eat their meals at their desk or in the kitchen where he could find someone if he needed them. And he made a point of interrupting lunches when too many people congregated in the kitchen so the team had learned ways to...

"Where the hell are all my pens?" someone yelled down the hallway.

Cricket heard the bellow and had to work hard to keep herself from bursting out with laughter. Debbie was still standing in her doorway but, thankfully, was looking in the direction of the yelling so Cricket had time to compose her features into an expression of concern and confusion.

"What?" Debbie whispered as she squinted in the direction from which the bellow had come. "Not again!" she giggled then quickly covered her face with her hands to keep their boss from seeing her laughter at his expense. Debbie turned back to Cricket, a huge grin on her pixie-like features. "Oh, this is too good! After yesterday afternoon's staff meeting, he deserves much more than someone stealing all of his..."

"And how the hell did all of my pictures get turned upside down?" the man yelled again to no one in particular.

Debbie stepped inside Cricket's office so their boss didn't see her laughing. "This is perfect," she laughed, covering her mouth with one hand while the other held her stomach as both women laughed at the latest joke at their boss' expense. "Who would think to turn the man's pictures upside down?" she burst out.

Cricket felt that it was now safe to release her laughter and went right along with Debbie as they both laughed while their boss, Jason Moran, stomped through the hallways on his rampage, trying to figure out who could have done something like this to his office. The man had accused several employees of disturbing his office over the past several months but since normally only his pens were stolen, the police wouldn't even get involved. "This is not funny!" he growled when he stomped passed Cricket's doorway and caught the two of them, as well as several other people, laughing in the hallways.

"Whoever did this," he called out to everyone in general, "you're fired! You hear me? You're fired!"

He walked into his office and slammed the door while the rest of the staff scurried away, still snickering at the mischief maker's bravery and creativity. Of course, that was before their boss let loose his wrath on everyone over the next few hours. He dumped the contents of the coffee pot down the drain and refused to let anyone make another pot or leave the office to grab their caffeine jolt at the deli in the lobby of the stairs. He also tossed papers across the conference room table when someone was trying to make a proposal about how to resolve an issue in the office, he stormed through the office stealing everyone else's pens and dumped them into their garbage cans. It was a highly ineffective retaliation since everyone simply picked their pens out of their trashcans again after he left their office but it was still demoralizing.

By the time he left for his lunch meeting, Cricket was feeling bad about what she'd done. Normally, Jason simply yelled and growled about her antics. He'd never actually made people more miserable as he had today. But apparently he was on a rampage to find out who was stealing his ball point pens and turning his cheap artwork upside down.

Cricket frowned throughout the morning while doing the data entry that was her job. She was on her last expense report when Debbie and two other co-workers stepped into her office.

"Coast clear?" Cricket asked with relish, more than ready to get out of this horrible environment.

"All clear. He left five minutes ago. We're actually one of the last to leave for lunch so grab your purse and let's go," Debbie urged.

"Did you hear that Mona and Jeff both quit this morning?" Debbie announced, shaking her head because probably the entire staff felt the same way.

Josie rolled her eyes at the loss. "We're more insulated from his wrath because he doesn't believe anyone here in the accounting department has any kind of imagination. We're just boring data entry clerks in his mind."

Cricket listened to their comments but didn't hesitate to log out of her computer for a break. She grabbed her purse and the four women were out the door, eagerly rushing towards the elevators. "Where are we going?" Cricket asked, thinking just a simple sandwich would suffice. She preferred to be back before Jason returned, not wanting to hear him growl about how his staff went out to lunch right after he did. In his mind, he's paying everyone so, therefore, his staff should work harder than he does.

Josie clapped her hands as an idea occurred to her. "Let's spoil ourselves and hit Antoine's for lunch. Anyone up for something decadent and fattening?"

"I'm all for that. Why don't we only order appetizers and desserts so we're all slow this afternoon with a sugar coma?" Debbie suggested.

Cricket smiled, more than ready to eat just about anything. She'd had to rush this morning in order to make it to the parking garage in time. She'd woken up fifteen minutes late and, instead of just arriving a few minutes late for work or, more specifically, late to see her mystery man, she'd skipped breakfast.

She smiled while she stood behind the three other women as she remembered the thrill she'd experienced when she'd arrived just in time to walk to the building while the stranger watched her. Then it occurred to her how crazy her life had become since the first time she'd seen the handsome man. Was she really cutting out food so she could arrive in time to get her adrenaline rush now?

She bit her lip and nodded to herself. Yes, she really was.

But who could blame her? The man was hot! She could berate herself all she wanted in her mind, but the truth was, his gaze across the courtyard was definitely the thrill of her day.

"Let's go," Josie called out as soon as the elevator doors opened. "I'm starving." Debbie, Josie and Allyson all chatted among themselves, trying to include Cricket in their conversation but since they were discussing husbands, children and babies, Cricket couldn't really contribute much since she didn't know anything about that aspect of life. The elegant restaurant was only a block and a half away from their office, but it was one of those exclusive places which meant it wasn't normally in the price range of four lowly accountants. So this was a real treat and much better than a deli sandwich or the burgers at Durango's where they normally grabbed lunch.

The four women were seated immediately since Allyson, the fourth member of their group, was dating one of the waiters at the restaurant. She might be divorced with two kids, but she still had an active eye for the men. The four women smiled excitedly as they took their seats among Chicago's elite. These were the power brokers, the wealthy patrons of the arts and the controllers of money. Bankers, successful entrepreneurs, wealthy tourists and anyone who wanted to be seen showed up at Antoine's for lunch. In another two hours, the powerful wives of Chicago would arrive in droves for their afternoon tea and brandy and two hours after that, the martini crowd would press together in the bar, eager to be seen mingling among the other patrons at the exclusive restaurant.

As the four of them were seated, Allyson's boyfriend came by and told them what to order since there weren't any prices on the menu. He handed each of them water with cucumber slices, then walked away to let them decide on their meals and to help his other tables.

The ladies sipped their water, excited to be a part of this daily spectacle. Well, three of them were, at least. Cricket sipped her water, but she didn't ooh and ahh at the people around them. She knew several of them by reputation, but her mind was also doing an inventory of their assets. Not their bank accounts, but their art and jewelry collections.

Other people might not have that kind of knowledge, but Cricket hadn't come from a normal family. Her father was one of the best art thieves in the world, and her mother was one of three thieves internationally who could relieve owners of just about any piece of jewelry she wanted, any time she wanted.

Of course, neither her mother nor her father ever kept their stolen pieces. At least, Cricket didn't think they kept any of it.

She shook her head as she contemplated the possibility. No, the absolute rule with thieves was to never hold onto anything one didn't want to lose. There was always someone coming up through the ranks who was more daring, more skillful with the latest technology, or more stealthy at removing others' possessions. Why would a thief trust a security system that they easily knew how to circumvent?

The other never-break rule was…Don't Get Caught.

So far, neither parent had ever been caught, thankfully. But Cricket lived in fear of her father attempting a "project" (his term, not hers) that would be more of a trap than a heist. The police knew of her father, but they'd never been able to pin anything to him. He was more of a ghost or a legend in the art thieves' community than anyone else. The police still didn't understand how he'd done many of the heists he'd accomplished and he took pride in no one knowing how or, even sometimes, when he'd done a job. He only pulled the riskiest jobs and only if he knew he could get rid of the loot quickly. If a thief was caught, it was harder for the authorities to prove guilt if the evidence was no longer in their possession.

So although Cricket didn't actually steal anything, she'd grown up in a family that lived for the next job, thrived on the exhilaration of an anticipated heist. And she'd been taught all the tricks of the trade in the hopes of her joining the family business once she was old enough.

She hated stealing though. Just the idea of stealing something of value made her stomach turn over. She wasn't afraid of the risk. In fact, she loved the risk, the thrill of the challenge and the adventure, not to mention the incredible self-discipline needed to learn the intricate skills of the art of thievery. The planning was always fascinating too, but she'd limited her missions to the more mundane pen-stealing or office altering achievements.

No, the stress of getting caught as well as the guilt over taking something that wasn't hers definitely wasn't worth it. She only wanted the thrill, not the risk.

"Oh my goodness!" Josie gasped. "Isn't that the President of the United States over there?" she asked, pointing towards a table in the corner that was surrounded by stern looking men and women, all wearing sunglasses with what looked to be ear pieces for surreptitious communication.

Cricket turned to look, as did the two other women. There was a communal gasp when they realized that it was indeed the president. Cricket even groaned when she realized that the president was lunching with none other than her handsome mystery man. How was that possible? The man worked here in Chicago, what business would the president have with anyone here?

Okay, so Antoine's was the best restaurant in the city. And it was close to their office, just down the block in fact.

But really, the President? That just put her mystery man further out of her league. And a dangerous person for her to associate with. Her family history and a powerful, well connected man were not a mixture that worked well for any kind of long term relationship.

Not that she had any chance of a relationship with a man like that anyway. He probably dated more glamorous women. She'd most likely been mistaken when she'd thought he was going to talk to her in the deli that day. A man like that did not approach a woman like her. She was too mousy, too boring. She was an accountant, for goodness sake! He probably dated models or society women!

She turned around, feeling despondent all of a sudden, and faced her menu. "I think I'm going to order a burger and horrify the chef," she said, trying to throw off her sadness.

Thankfully, the other three turned back to the table, knowing that this was as close as they would get to the lofty man. It was pointless to ogle.

Unfortunately, that didn't stop her from gawking. The man wasn't directly in her line of vision, but if she turned her head just slightly to the right, she saw him. Everyone in the restaurant saw him because he was with the president, but she had eyes only for him.

It seemed like every time she looked in that direction, he was looking directly back at her. It was more than a little disconcerting and she actually had no idea what they ate for lunch. She went through the motions, but by the time Allyson's boyfriend was taking their plates away, she couldn't have named a single thing that had been in front of her for almost the past hour.

Her heart was pounding and she looked up again, her eyes colliding with his. He looked to almost be ignoring the president as he stared right back at her.

"You're awfully quiet," Josie said and Cricket's attention snapped right back to her co-workers. They'd all relished the meal that had apparently been above and beyond their expectations.

"Is the president really that fascinating?" Debbie asked. All of them had noticed her lack of attention during the meal. "And are you okay? You look flushed. Maybe you're coming down with something?"

Josie smiled and wiggled her eyebrows. "It isn't our illustrious leader that has Cricket so distracted."

Debbie and Allyson both turned their heads and caught the president walking out while he said something to a taller man. "Oh…!" Debbie said with a sigh as she realized who Cricket had been looking at. "That's the dreamy guy who works in the building across the courtyard, isn't it?" she asked, sighing with happiness as the man disappeared out of the restaurant.

Josie and Debbie both turned their heads, trying to see him one more time, but by then he was already out the door, only the last few secret service agents scanning the room giving any indication that it hadn't been their imagination about the president being in the same dining room with them.

"Come to think of it," Josie said, "I think I've seen him too."

"He's just the guy that works in the other building," Cricket said again. "I'm sure he's very nice but I didn't get a good look at him." She wasn't really lying, even though she'd been sneaking peeks at him all through the meal.

Allyson looked at her watch. "We'd better head back and forget about the tall, dark and handsome stranger Cricket is drooling over," she teased. "Mr. Moran is bound to be back and furious with his staff for taking a legally allotted lunch period."

The four women nodded their concurrence and started taking out their wallets. But before anyone could pull out cash or credit card, their waiter arrived magically at their table. He put a hand to Allyson's shoulder affectionately as he said, "You're check has been taken care of, ladies."

All four of them stared at him with their mouths open. "Excuse me?" Cricket asked, confused.

"A man took care of your check already," he repeated. "I don't know by whom, but my boss took your bill and told me to tell all of you that it was paid." He shrugged and winked at Allyson before moving off to his next table, eager to earn tips from the lunch crowd.

They sat there in stunned silence for a long moment, each of them processing the news. Then one by one, they turned to look at Cricket and smiled as the realization came upon them. "It was him!" Allyson hissed excitedly. "You somehow got that hottie to pay for your meal and we all benefitted!"

Josie and Debbie were all grinning from ear to ear, laughing when Cricket blushed painfully. "I doubt he would do that for us. I don't even know who he is."

"Why not?" Josie asked. "You and he were exchanging those heated glances all during the meal. Good grief, you barely ate anything because you were too focused on him!"

The three of them laughed as she blushed painfully but Cricket simply shook her head. "It was probably Allyson's boyfriend being nice."

"Uh huh," they each said almost in unison, none of them actually believing it. But they knew they had a limited amount of time before their boss came back and they had to be at their desks, looking busy before that happened. So they all grabbed their purses and coats, rushed out of the restaurant, and hurried down the sidewalk. The afternoon wind had turned colder over the past hour, typical of this time of the year in Chicago. With the lake just a block away, the wind could pick up unexpectedly and bring along with it a painful chill. It was also why Chicago got more snow than many parts of the country, but not nearly as much snow as Buffalo or central New York areas.

They all hurried into the building, bundling into the elevator and laughing at how quickly the weather changed. By the time they reached their floor, their faces were grim, all traces of relaxation from their break gone as they once again faced the work on their respective desks.

"I'm going job hunting," Josie whispered as they walked down the depressing hallways. "Jason might pay higher salaries, but nothing is worth this much irritation."

"I'm with you," Allyson said as she ducked into her office.

"Count me in," Debbie called back as she went into her office as well.

None of them realized that Cricket was silent. She definitely wanted a new job, but if she didn't work here, she would miss her morning "meeting".

How ridiculous was that? She sat down at her desk and told herself firmly that she was definitely going to have to find a new job. She'd start the search tonight. The man might be tempting, but her friends were right. This was not a good work environment. She needed something new. With any luck, she'd find a fabulous job right here in the building and she'd still get to see her mystery man every day.

CHAPTER 4

Ryker watched the blond woman across the restaurant, more convinced than ever that he was going to meet the lovely lady from across the courtyard. She was sitting primly at her table during lunch, looking serenely beautiful. Her friends were giggling about something, but Ryker noticed that his lovely lady only smiled weakly at whatever they were discussing. Probably because she was more focused on peering in his direction than she was in paying attention to the lunch conversation. Even Ryker was distracted from his conversation with the President because he kept trying to catch her eye.

Thankfully, the President knew exactly what was going on. "I can see that global politics and the national legal system are poor competition compared to the blond beauty across the room."

Ryker laughed even though he'd been caught being rude. The President wasn't one to hold a grudge though and he even approved. "What's her name?" he asked, changing the subject since there was little chance he could get Ryker to focus on accepting a federal judgeship.

"I don't know yet," Ryker replied, a possessive feeling coming to him at that moment. "Is it that obvious?" Ryker asked, cringing inside at how unfocused he'd been. He prided himself on his discipline but there was something about that woman that just got to him.

"Just a bit. But only because I've known you for so long."

After that, they discussed personal issues which were easier to follow, allowing Ryker to use most of his brain power to think of ways to meet his lovely lady. Unfortunately, he had a meeting right after lunch that he had to hurry back to the office for. He walked out with the President, shaking hands with him before the man ducked into his armored limousine and sped away out of sight.

Ryker was about to go back to the office, but he had a thought and went back into the restaurant. Whispering something to the waiter, he pointed to the table where his lady was sitting, giving him instructions to take care of their lunch tab.

Walking back to his office, he smiled to himself. She might not have been sitting across the table from him, but at least he got to pay for her lunch. That was something, he told himself. It was odd, but he wasn't normally attracted to women who were shy. He typically preferred the more aggressive, confident women. That was probably because he didn't normally have time to waste on chasing women. Besides, they generally seemed to do the chasing and he either accepted their offers or passed, not really bothered either way.

This woman was different. There was just something about her that made him place her in a distinctive category. He probably should have gone over to her table and offered his business card, asked her to give him a call when it was convenient.

On second thought, she probably wouldn't have called him. He knew that she was interested, but she wouldn't even look him in the eye except when it was by accident. So he would have to get her information first, figure out what she liked and pursue her with a bit more flair and patience.

Back at his desk, he was going through several reports when Joan interrupted him to announce his next appointment had arrived. Ryker looked at the name and sighed, wishing he'd canceled the meeting. He didn't want to deal with this man today, he thought as the door to his office burst open and a short, rotund man with a badly receding hairline came into view.

"Good afternoon, Jason," Ryker said, standing up and moving around to the other side of the desk to shake the shorter man's hand. Ryker wasn't a huge fan of Jason Moran, but he was a client. At least for now. The man was a blowhard who originally thought he could order Ryker around. The first time Jason had done this, Ryker had politely walked him out of the office, shaking his hand at the elevator door and told him that he didn't think The Thorpe Group was the kind of law firm that would be of service to Jason's company.

The man quickly realized his mistake and it hadn't ever happened again. Since that day, Jason Moran had been charm personified around this office. But Ryker knew that the man abused his staff, and he didn't like that. He was tempted to tell the man to find another lawyer, but he hadn't yet made up his mind. Perhaps this visit would tilt the decision one way or another. Ryker found that he didn't have the patience to deal with clients he didn't respect. And since he didn't need to deal with the little man, he had no qualms about either eliminating the man from their client list, or pushing him off to one of his junior associates.

"Thanks for seeing me on such short notice. I know you're extremely busy." Jason took the liberty of sitting down before Ryker even offered him a seat.

Ryker remained standing, telling the shorter man in no uncertain terms what Ryker thought of Jason's manners. "My assistant mentioned you need some help urgently."

Jason flushed, knowing that Ryker Thorpe was one of those powerful men in Chicago a business owner didn't want to mess with. The man might be a lawyer who was probably always on the lookout for clients, but Ryker Thorpe had many powerful friends. One didn't want to insult him. Jason knew he'd done that during his first appointment and had worked hard to maintain a polite demeanor ever since. But it was hard. As far as Jason was concerned, Ryker Thorpe was paid by Jason, therefore the man should act like an employee.

That wasn't the way things worked, at least not where The Thorpe Brothers were concerned. Having Ryker Thorpe, or any Thorpe brother, as one's lawyer, pretty much pushed away most legal issues. Their reputation for winning just about any case they took on was legendary. The Thorpe Group's rates might be twice as high as other lawyers, maybe even three times the going rate, but they also eliminated most legal issues from even happening. Either by their reputation, or by offering sound, legal advice in advance so one didn't get into legal messes in the first place.

Unfortunately, this wasn't one of those situations that might have been avoided with legal advice. This was almost personal now. "I have a huge problem," Jason started out, wishing he could stand up, but also knowing that it wouldn't do any good since Ryker Thorpe was almost a foot taller. Jason knew he would still feel small and inferior so he remained seated. At least he could enjoy the ultra-soft sofa while feeling small!

"And that would be?' Ryker prompted, smothering his impatience. He glanced at his watch, knowing that he had another appointment in ten minutes. He'd only squeezed Moran in now so he wouldn't have to endure his presence for a longer period of time later on.

Jason rubbed his forehead, almost embarrassed now to discuss the issue. But he had no clue how to stop the problem. "I have someone breaking into my office on a regular basis. I need help catching the thief."

Ryker tried to keep his facial expression blank, but he was having a hard time hiding his surprise. This wasn't really a legal issue. Was the man wasting his time in addition to being an irritation? "Have you spoken to the police?" Ryker asked, wondering how he could help. "If you catch the person, I can represent your interests. But until then, I'm not sure how I can assist you."

Jason grimaced, his irritation getting the better of him now that he was thinking back to his problem instead of focusing on being polite. "You have investigators, don't you?" Jason snapped. Then calmed down when he caught Ryker's dark scowl. "Sorry. This has been plaguing me for a while. The police won't help me because they say nothing of value has been stolen and I can't even prove that it wasn't an employee playing a prank on me. They said it was an internal issue and if I wanted to stop the thefts, I'd have to discuss the issue with my employees. I don't know who else to turn to. I've hired a private investigator, but they haven't been able to stop the guy for the past four break-ins."

That was a surprise. And confusing. What kind of pranks would be played in an office environment? He knew that his staff had some office betting going on. In fact, even he had some private bets on the problem between his brother and their office manager. But he didn't really consider an office betting pool to be a prank. And no one stole anything. At least nothing that had been reported. Office pencils, pens, paper clips, envelopes and small items were obtained for personal use all the time, but that wasn't really theft in his mind. He considered it more along the lines of "the cost of doing business" and not a crime. "What is this person stealing?" Ryker asked, intrigued despite the arrogant man.

Jason sighed and rubbed the back of his neck. "Pens," he said, smothering his mouth with his hand.

Ryker stood still, deciphering the man's words. "I'm sorry, Jason, but did you just tell me that the thief is stealing pens?"

Jason nodded, looking down at the floor.

Ryker watched carefully, wondering if Jason was going to offer any additional information. "Are they expensive pens?" he prompted when the exasperating man remained silent.

"No!" Jason almost yelled, standing up and starting to pace through the office that was more than twice the size of his own. "In fact, that's what's so infuriating about the issue. There was a two hundred dollar pen on my desk last night but whoever broke into my office only stole all my cheap, ball point pens. About ten of them!"

Ryker stared, shocked and amused. "So this is more of a practical joke?" he offered, trying to get to the heart of the issue.

"It's a pain in my ass!" Jason came back. Then rubbed his face and neck once more. "I just want to find the bastard who is doing this and make it stop!" He paced back and forth then threw his hands up in the air in exasperation. "And last night, all of my paintings were…" he hesitated.

Ryker stood up straighter, starting to realize that there was more of a crime here when artwork was involved. "Stolen?" he suggested.

Jason shook his head, his face turning beet red with embarrassment. "They were pinned upside down."

Ryker almost laughed, both at the idea of someone messing with the man's head like this, and the obnoxious man's irritation at the culprit's antics. "Well, that's…." Ryker hesitated, not sure how to diplomatically describe Jason's issue. "Problematic," he finally finished.

Jason was too angry to notice Ryker's amusement. "You're damn right it is! But here's the thing," he finally said, putting his hands on his hips, mimicking Ryker's pose. "You have a great team of investigators. I've heard you've deployed them for your clients on numerous occasions. I'm asking for your help with this issue now."

Ryker leaned against the back of the chair, considering the man's request. He finally said, "I think the police are right in this case. It sounds more like a personnel issue than a legal issue, Jason. If these antics are going on in your office, have you questioned your staff? Are they happy and ready to work or are they angry at some benefit that is being eliminated from their package? Or are salaries down?" Ryker knew that many times people got back at their employers in creative ways. But stealing pens? "These kinds of things sound like someone who is just working late and snuck into your office."

"It can't be an employee," he grumbled, looking like he was at his wits end because of this situation. "Since this started, I've put in a new security system, installed new measures, put in cameras, electrical monitoring devices, badging equipment. Every time there is a break-in, I call my security firm and demand them to fix my security so the break-ins will stop but this guy is able to circumvent everything my security people put in. And there's no trace of anything. The police dusted for fingerprints but found nothing. And they said the same thing you did so they aren't willing to investigate any further." Jason took a deep breath. "Look, I know this isn't really your area, but I also know your investigator, Mark, and his team are great at finding out things. I don't want to know how they do it. I just want to find out who is pulling these pranks or thefts or whatever you want to call them and make it all stop." The man took a deep breath and rubbed his hand over his face. "I'm looking like a fool and I don't like that. Not one little bit!"

Ryker considered the man's request and actually started to feel sorry for him. He was right. These kinds of things did make a boss look foolish and disrespected. It would eventually create fallout in decreased business and he'd have to lay people off. So in the end, Ryker agreed to help out not so much for Jason's sake but to keep all those people employed. "How about if I speak with Mark and ask him how he can help? If there is anything he can do, I'll have him get in contact with you. Will that work?"

Jason breathed a sigh of relief. At least there was hope, he thought.

"That sounds fair," he replied and puffed up, relieved that he was getting some help. Shaking Ryker's hand, Jason wished he could walk down the hallway to this mysterious Mark's office and demand a consultation. But Jason also knew that wasn't the way The Thorpe Group operated. Jason would wait around and this Mark fellow would give him a call.

At least the company was customer oriented so it wouldn't be a long wait. But any sort of wait, in Jason's mind, was irritating. He wasn't a patient kind of man. When he wanted something, he wanted it done yesterday.

Walking out, he crossed the courtyard slowly, wishing he could think of another way to deal with the situation. In the end, he knew he'd just have to wait for Mark's call.

Ryker walked down the hallway to Mark's office as soon as Jason Moran left. "Do you have a moment?" Ryker asked.

Mark turned to face his boss, forcing his mind away from the six computer screens that were mounted in a row and on top of each other for easier viewing. "Sure, boss. What's up?"

Ryker quickly explained Jason's problem, smiling as soon as Mark laughed out loud. In the end Mark said, "I'll give him a call as soon as I get this report down to Axel. Maybe there's something I can do."

"That's all I can ask," he said and walked out, heading out of the building and to his lunch appointment.

Later that evening, he left the office in a hurry to get to a business dinner that he was not looking forward to. He'd agreed to take Xander's place tonight because Xander got caught up in a meeting. But all he wanted to do now was head home and relax with the football game on.

Then he saw her. She was leaving the office with her coat wrapped around her tightly to ward off the cold wind that had picked up earlier in the day. The sun had already set but the lights of the courtyard as well as the headlights of the other vehicles that were exiting the parking garage made it easy to see everything around.

He watched for only a moment before he made a decision. Ryker hadn't made it this far by letting any opportunity slip out of his grasp.

Walking towards her at a perfect intercept angle, he made for his target. He also knew the exact moment when she realized he was coming towards her. It was fairly evident that she recognized him. It was in her eyes, in the way her body tensed and her cheeks turned a lovely shade of pink.

"Good evening," he said, smoothly adjusting their positions so they were out of the line of employee traffic heading towards the parking garage, eager to get home to their families. "I'm Ryker Thorpe," he said, extending his hand, taking her smaller one in his. "I've seen you over at the other building in the mornings. Since we've seen each other so often, I thought it was past time to introduce ourselves. Maybe you'd even let me buy you a cup of coffee? Or dinner sometime?" he asked.

Cricket couldn't stop the trembling. It was one thing to see this man across the courtyard. It was a completely different issue to see him up close and personal like this. He was taller than she'd anticipated. And bigger! The man had muscles upon muscles underneath that suit. Her mother had been an excellent teacher at being able to spot faux anything and this man's shoulders were not padded with fluff. Only muscle.

"Um…" she stammered, feeling ridiculous. Her mother would be outraged by her lack of finesse. "I'm Cricket Fairchild," she finally was able to say, looking down and wishing she could extricate her hand from his. "I really have to go," she said. "I need to get home to…." she couldn't think of a valid reason why she needed to hurry home other than to escape this man's enigmatic and terrifying closeness that had her knees wobbling and her heart fluttering like she was experiencing her first eighth grade crush.

Ryker smiled, tucking her arm onto his elbow. "We're heading in the same direction so I'll walk you to your car. That will give you time to tell me how you got the name Cricket."

Cricket couldn't help but smile. Most people made some irritating reference to a bug. His comment was close, but it was much nicer. So was his smile. Those icy blue eyes were more than a little intimidating, but if she just looked at his chin or his nose, she could think a bit more coherently.

"My parents are a bit unorthodox. Apparently, a picnic was involved."

They were out on the street, walking down the sidewalk by this point. She saw her friends turn the corner, all of them rushing to get home to their families. Cricket didn't blame them. If she had this man to rush home to, she'd be scurrying along as well. After such a trying day, everyone in the office felt a strong need to head home and hug their children or their husbands before settling down to a nice, relaxing glass of wine.

"I thought ants were the main irritant at a picnic," he commented.

Cricket laughed. "My parents really don't do anything in the normal manner."

"What do they do?" he asked, instantly curious and enjoying the walk more than he thought he would. He had that business dinner that started in less than thirty minutes but for the first time in his life, he wanted to relax with a female instead of hurrying off to resolve some legal or business issue.

When her hand went up, waving about in the cool, autumn air, Ryker knew that she was going to try and either lie, or pass off the question. "Oh, they don't have any particular profession that they talk about," she said.

Her comment instantly raised his curiosity. "What kind of profession do they not talk about?" he asked.

Cricket couldn't believe how perceptive the man was. Normally her comment made people think that her parents were ultra-rich, or dirt poor. Either they didn't discuss their business interests because it was considered crass to do so, or they didn't have any business interests to discuss.

With this man's comment, she couldn't help but laugh. "You don't allow any ambiguity, do you?" she asked carefully.

He smiled, charmed by her smile and fascinated by the glint in her clear, green eyes. "And you are still avoiding the question. Which means that your parents are either very naughty, or embarrassingly wealthy. Which is it?"

Cricket didn't know that her green eyes were sparkling as she considered ways to answer his question without giving anything away. "That only tells me that you are a very cynical man. Does everyone have to have a secret? Or hide their parents away? Why can't I just be one of those women who don't have parents any longer? Or maybe I had a tough upbringing and I just don't talk about my parents in any way?"

They'd reached the courtyard already and Ryker was even more intrigued. Never had any woman so effectively avoided answering his questions before. Most of the women of his acquaintance were more than eager to brag about their familial associations, thinking he cared about that kind of thing. He didn't, but something about the way this lovely woman with the honey glints of her hair sparkling in the overhead lights made him think that the woman had more secrets than the FBI. And he intended to find out all of them.

"Have dinner with me tonight," he commanded, keeping her hand tucked on his elbow even while she tried to pull it away. He didn't care about the business dinner he was supposed to attend. The hell with them, he thought. He'd never missed a business meeting before, but if this woman would agree to dinner with him, he'd blow it all off in order to unravel her mysteries.

Cricket smiled, instantly flattered, but still not willing to agree to dinner tonight. "Give me your card and I'll call you." It was the best way she'd learned to push men away when she didn't want any further communication with them. Unfortunately, she didn't want to get to know this man. She preferred the fantasy because the reality was terrifying!

Ryker considered her request for all of a fraction of a second. "No you won't," he said with a shake of his head. "You'll walk away from me and won't call me. Then I'll have to stalk you out here in the courtyard every day. But you'll probably shift your schedule now that we've met."

Her green eyes widened at his accurate assessment of her plans. "If I promise to call?" she laughed, caught in her own trap. He was right. She wouldn't have called him back. The man was completely charming, amazingly sexy and totally out of her league. She knew she would be much more comfortable feeling the zing of his gaze from afar.

Ryker shook his head. He reached into his breast pocket and extracted a leather case, pulling a white business card out. "You won't. But here's my card anyway. I dare you to call me," he teased. "And if you don't, I'm not worried. I have my ways of finding people," he promised ominously.

Cricket's nervousness increased tenfold with his words. She took the card and spun around on her heel, almost running into the parking garage in a sudden, desperate need to get away from this strange, shockingly direct and amazingly sexy man.

She walked to her car and slipped in behind the wheel, feeling a little like Alice in Wonderland. The world was definitely topsy-turvy when she was walked out of work with a man who dined with the President of the United States!

Goodness, her father would break down with a stroke if he ever found out about Ryker Thorpe's interest!

CHAPTER 5

Cricket's whole body stiffened at the sound of the doorbell ringing. She looked up from her mystery novel, her eyes staring at the door as if she could somehow see through the wood. She had only one deadbolt on the door, knowing that it was too easy to break through elaborate security systems so why bother?

But now, hearing the doorbell ring and thinking of the stranger's ice blue eyes, she wished she had something that could more effectively lock him out of her house.

It had taken her over an hour to calm down after their brief conversation earlier tonight. She'd been so excited and flustered, she'd almost taken the wrong roads home!

Maybe it wasn't him. Maybe she'd just been thinking about him so much lately that he was on her mind. So when the doorbell rang, she'd just assumed it was the man. Maybe it was one of her neighbors. Maybe Jennie next door needed a babysitter because her husband was late coming home from work and she needed to go out for some reason. Or perhaps it was Leandra across the street coming to return the baking dish she'd borrowed last week.

Cricket continued to stare at the door, flinching when the doorbell rang once again because she hadn't opened it.

With growing trepidation, she walked over to the doorway. She knew with absolute certainty that she wasn't going to see her baking dish tonight, nor was she going to get to play Candyland with toddlers.. No, the person on the other side of that slab of wood was her stranger, the man with the strange, scary eyes. The man she skipped breakfast in order to see in the morning.

The man who terrified her as no one else ever could.

Her fingers trembled as she laid her hand down on the craftsman style door knob, taking a deep breath before she twisted the cold metal. Every part of her mind listened to the door opening. The slight squeak as the deadbolt was released, the scrape as the door tumblers retracted and the swish while the air shifted with the door opening.

"I thought you'd never answer the door," Ryker Thorpe's deep, hypnotic voice said.

Cricket shivered with the sound, her mind saying the words over and over again. "I knew it would be you," she whispered, her breath caught in her throat and her eyes wide with fascination at the handsome, amazingly virile man standing on her doorstep.

"Were you expecting someone else?" he asked, smiling at how cute she looked as she peered out of her doorway. She looked warm and cozy, like she'd been under a blanket reading a book.

Cricket didn't want him to think that and she quickly shook her head. "Not at all!"

"Good. Then I'm not interrupting anything?"

She grinned despite her nervousness. "Can I help you?" she asked. She held her breath, hoping anxiously he wasn't here to just sell her a magazine subscription or something similarly tedious.

"You can open the door and let me in," the man's voice replied. He was leaning against the door jamb, looking smooth and ultra-sophisticated with the expensive suit loose around his flat stomach, his five-hundred dollar tie gone and the top buttons of his Indian cotton shirt opened at the his neck.

Good grief, she even thought his neck was sexy!

She sighed with exasperation at herself, wondering why she was so wary of this man. She met men all the time. She avoided bars because men hit on her constantly. So it was almost annoying that this man didn't irritate her like the other men. She had a defense set up for when the men hit on her but she knew that she was defenseless around this man. Her face turned embarrassingly pink and her nerves did something she didn't want to even try to describe.

She bit her lip, wondering how she was going to get out of this mess. "I don't know."

Ryker smiled, relaxing since she hadn't slammed the door in his face. "Aren't you interested to know why I'm here?" he asked.

Cricket bit her lower lip, trying to decide how much she feared this man, and how much of her fear was unrealistic.

"I don't think I should care why you are here," she replied with complete honesty and the hint of a shy smile.

He chuckled, the deep sound making her heart flicker more quickly.

"That's an honest answer, at least." He straightened his shoulders and stood up; Cricket suddenly realized how small she really was compared to Ryker Thorpe.

"How about if I come bearing gifts?" he offered and raised the bottle of wine he'd brought from his wine cellar. He'd called Xander and discussed the business dinner he'd agreed to go to earlier. But when Xander told him the whole story, they both agreed that it wasn't absolutely necessary for a representative of The Thorpe Group show up at this particular function so here he was, hoping to have a quiet evening with the lovely Cricket Fairchild.

Cricket inhaled sharply when she read the wine label, her eyes snapping back up into his ice blue eyes, wishing he'd brought something other than wine. Wine was her kryptonite! And when she dared to glance downward, she gasped audibly as she read the label. "That's cheating!" she said with her eyebrows low over her eyes. Palmer 2009 Margaux was one of the great wines of that year. And she loved wine! She rarely drank wine because she couldn't afford the good stuff on her salary but her mother had taught her to truly appreciate the thrilling intensity and burst of flavors in a good wine.

Ryker put his palm to the door and gently pushed. "I'm coming in, Cricket," he said softly, his ice blue eyes never leaving her worried, green ones, watching for any sign of resistance. But she couldn't push him out. And it had nothing to do with the fabulous bottle of wine he held in his hand.

It had everything to do with the magical feeling she was experiencing as the man pushed his way into her house. She'd thought he was exceptionally handsome from across the courtyard. And today in the courtyard as he'd walked her to her car, he'd been shockingly forward, a character trait she generally didn't like. But in this man, it seemed to fit. Now, with him standing here, his height and broad shoulders making her feel small and feminine, she couldn't deny him entry. There was something about him that called to her like no other man ever had.

"Wine glasses?" he prompted when she just stood there in her foyer.

Cricket jumped, embarrassed that she'd just been standing there staring at the man's shoulders, and pulled her eyes away. "Yes! Wine glasses!" She spun around, surprised that she'd actually forgotten about the wine, his entire entry strategy. She never forgot about wine!

She moved off to the kitchen, trying to get her mind back in gear. "How did you know where I lived?" she asked as she reached up and pulled down two wine glasses from the cabinet over her fridge. They were dusty from lack of use so she cleaned them both in the sink, afraid to look into the window in front of her. It was dark outside which made the window like a mirror and she'd probably drop her wine glasses if he caught her eye in the window right at this moment.

Ryker watched with growing interest as the woman stretched up, her soft, pink sweater moving along with her arms to reveal pale skin on her back and allowing him an unlimited view of her adorable backside. It was round and firm, pressing against the black slacks she'd worn to work that morning. Her pink sweater was still on, but it wasn't pulled over her slacks any longer. He suspected she didn't even realize how adorable she looked, all frazzled and rumpled. He was used to seeing her looking perfectly coifed and walking with professional determination. He liked this look. She was much more appealing. And definitely sexier.

She spun around with the now-sparkling glasses, her eyes sliding reluctantly up to his and he wanted to kiss her. He wanted to see what she would feel like with those soft, full breasts pressed against his chest, her warm sighs blowing against his neck. And his body reacted instantly to the image.

She waited expectantly, glancing from his eyes to the bottle. When she realized what he was thinking, her heart sped up and she felt her cheeks heat. "Oh," she sighed and almost forgot about the glasses in her hand.

Ryker knew he was making her even more nervous. That hadn't been his intention but the woman was incredibly sexy standing there looking confused. He smiled and relented slightly. "Bottle opener?" he asked.

Again, her whole body jerked with the question and the realization that she was still staring at his mouth, almost begging the man to kiss her.

She shook her head and placed the glasses on the countertop behind her, almost smacking one of the stems off when she missed the counter because of her nervousness. Her fingers were clumsy as she rummaged around in her kitchen drawers. When she finally found her bottle opener, she swung around, holding the tool up victoriously.

"You found it," he said, amusement apparent in his eyes. "I take it you don't drink wine very often?" he asked as he opened the bottle with expertise.

She smiled and leaned against the counter, relieved that she finally had a break from trying to think for a few moments. "Not often, no."

"Are you a beer drinker?" he asked, pouring some wine into both glasses before handing her one.

"I enjoy the occasional beer," she said, accepting the glass with growing excitement. "But I'll admit, I'm a sucker for a good bottle of wine. Hence your presence in my kitchen," she grinned.

"Ouch!" he laughed and clinked her glass. "To finally meeting," he offered as a toast.

Cricket thought about that, then smiled and brought the glass to her nose. She took a long moment to enjoy the bouquet, letting the fruity scent fill her nostrils and enjoyment sensors. When she took the first sip, she let the wine slip slowly into her mouth, feeling the burst of flavor on her tongue, amazed by the incredible taste. "Oh my!" she sighed happily, her eyes still closed as she savored her first taste. "This is truly amazing."

Ryker watched as the woman he'd thought was the sexiest human being alive just blew him away with the most sensual image he'd ever seen in his life. He enjoyed wine just like the rest of the world. But watching Cricket Fairchild take her first sip of the Palmer Margaux had him aching to possess her. He wanted all of that passion, that erotic sensitivity, to be directed at him, or with him as he took her over the peak into sexual bliss.

He was standing about a foot away from her in the little periwinkle kitchen, his eyes looking at her strangely. The wine bottle was in one hand and his glass of wine in the other, but he was just standing there staring at her. "Aren't you going to try it?" she asked, looking up at him curiously.

Ryker blinked and glanced down at his glass. "I'm not sure I need to. Your enjoyment is much more interesting than anything I've ever seen," he said and watched with fascination as she blushed once again. He wondered if she sunburned or tanned. Probably the former with her fair skin, he thought, noting the platinum highlights in her hair. "So what do you do?" he asked, trying to change the subject so that she was more comfortable around him. He instinctively knew that he'd have to get her used to him before he could make a move on her and since he was aching to take her into his arms, he had to speed the "comfort" process along more quickly or he might just go up in flames with wanting her.

She led him out of the kitchen so they could be more comfortable in her little den. "I'm an accountant for Jason Moran's office."

That surprised him, knowing how Jason treated his staff. This woman didn't look like someone who would take a lot of verbal abuse. "And how do you like that work?" he asked, thinking that she didn't strike him as an accounting type. She looked more like a ballet dancer or a gourmet chef, someone with hidden passions and secrets that he wanted to discover.

Cricket shrugged her shoulder. "It pays the mortgage," she said and looked around at her tiny house. "It's small, but I love this house," she explained. There was only a family room and kitchen with a half bath downstairs and two small bedrooms upstairs, but it was hers. She paid the mortgage on it faithfully every month and kept meticulous records of her income and expenditures. She'd been taught as a kid that thieves could never own property; they had to be ready to leave at a moment's notice. She'd lived all over the world and could speak French, Italian and Spanish fluently, German well enough to get by, and a tad of Portuguese. But only because her mother and father had dragged her all over the world, following their next "project". Cricket had learned to adapt, to blend in and understand the culture of each city quickly, including absorbing the dialect and accents so people wouldn't think she was a stranger. Strangers were dangerous. Someone who "spoke the language" was a safer bet as a friend.

Ryker looked around as well, impressed with how cozy the room looked. It was as if there were a fire in the fireplace, but it was really just the warm hues and the soft lighting. She'd done a great job of decorating to make the area inviting and comfortable. "How long have you lived here?" he asked. And the conversation went on for hours. She curled up in her big chair with him across from her, relaxing as the wine crept into her bloodstream, making her more talkative than she normally would have been. He was a fascinating man, having visited almost all of the cities she'd been to and spoke several languages as well. By the end of the evening, she felt like she knew him a bit more thoroughly, but she never accepted that she might actually know his mind. This man was not like the one dimensional, easy going gentlemen she'd casually dated in the past. .

As they talked about art and history, college and their favorite foods, Cricket came to realize that Ryker Thorpe had so many facets to his complex personality. He was a fascinating man. She could honestly say she'd never met anyone more intelligent and well-educated than Ryker Thorpe, including her father which was saying a lot. Her father might not have attended college or a university, but he could argue right along with the best of them about any subject. He prided himself on reading as much as he could get his hands on, but the man sitting in her family room was much more well-read, able to converse on just about any subject. He even knew about art, which wasn't a topic most people excelled at.

Of course, she didn't go into much detail about her knowledge of art and art history, and she didn't even touch on her ability to spot real versus fake diamonds, much less pick out the most flawless diamond in any room at a glance. No, all the skills that had been passed on by her mother and father would only lead to questions. Questions she couldn't answer. Or at least shouldn't answer. The answers would raise too many other questions.

They'd finished the bottle of wine and Cricket smothered a yawn, not wanting him to see it because he'd probably get up and leave. But this time, she couldn't suppress it and he quickly glanced at his watch, realizing how late it had gotten. "I'd better let you get some sleep," Ryker said, standing up.

Cricket rose as well, feeling painfully disappointed that their time together was coming to an end. She wished she could think of something to make him stay, keep him talking to her. But now that they were closer, her mind just fizzled out.

"Well," she started off, hiding her hands behind her back, feeling as nervous and awkward as a sixteen year old on her first date all of a sudden. "Um…thank you for bringing the wine. It was exceptionally wonderful." There! That was a good way to clear the air and say goodbye. If she could just stay on this side of the coffee table, then she might not throw herself into his arms and beg him to kiss her goodnight.

Ryker could see right through her attempts and he wasn't going to allow her the chance. He'd wanted to kiss her the moment he walked into this house and he wasn't going to be able to do that if she stayed over there with the furniture in the way. "Walk me to the door," he commanded, not waiting for her to respond but reaching out and easily taking her hand, leading her towards her front door.

When they were standing there in the tiny foyer, Cricket's hands still held in his, she stared straight ahead, looking only at his chest. She couldn't look at his eyes, nor his mouth. If she looked at either, he would know how desperately she wanted to kiss him. How much she wanted him to just pull her into his arms and ravish her.

And how desperately she wished she were anyone else's daughter. Earlier today, she'd seen this man with The President of the United States. She now knew he was a lawyer, which meant he was an officer of the courts – just one step away from the police. A lawyer and a thief did not mix under any formula, she told herself firmly.

"Goodnight," she whispered, trying to hide the nervousness and sadness from her voice and her eyes.

Ryker wasn't going to be dismissed so easily. He knew that they both needed what was to come. Bending lower, he put a finger under her chin, lifting her face so she was looking at him. There in her eyes, he saw what he was looking for. The same need that was filling him.

And that was all the permission he needed. Bending lower, he took her lips in his, kissing her gently, slowly, teasing her into participating with the kiss. Cricket's breath came out in a low, shocked hiss as she looked up at him. But that only lasted for a fraction of a second before she lifted her mouth up again, silently asking him to continue kissing her. She knew it was wrong, that this could never go anywhere, but for this one moment, this one kiss, she was going to enjoy the feelings, the surprise and the amazement of how lovely and crazy she felt in this man's arms.

She didn't realize that her own arms had moved up his shoulders and were now wrapped around his neck or that her fingers were in his hair, feeling the surprisingly soft texture. There was a moment's spinning but then she felt the door on her back and realized that he'd spun them around so that she was pressed against the door with his body pressing against hers. She loved the way he felt, pressed her softness against him, gasping in shock and thrilling with the knowledge that she could do this to this strong, virile man. His hands had been on her waist but she shivered when she felt those hands move upwards, wrapping around her rib cage and she silently begged him to move higher.

Ryker had to mentally shake himself. This woman was so soft and sexy, all he wanted to do was continue kissing her just like this. He tried to stop, but then her hand touched his cheek and he was lost once again. Lifting her up, his hands moved down to her hips, pulling her legs so they were wrapped around his waist.

Cricket couldn't believe what was happening. Surely she wasn't doing this, she thought when he lifted his head up. Then the urge to touch his skin was overwhelming so she moved her hand out of his hair. Her fingers touched his hard jawline, riveted with the texture. It was rougher than she'd expected, more fascinating and hot to the touch. She didn't realize she was gasping for air or that her chest was heaving against his. All she knew was that her fingertips were on fire from the simple gesture against his skin. And then she really got lost. His hands were rough as he lifted her higher, his mouth ravaging hers and she needed more! It wasn't enough and she shifted her body, her head falling backwards when she felt that hardness…no, it wasn't on her stomach any longer it was…just….perfect! She thought that her eyes might be rolling back in her head with the waves of pleasure washing over her again and again but even that wasn't enough. Everything felt so good, every time he moved his hand, every place his hard, demanding lips touched just made her ache a little bit more. She'd never experienced anything like his touch or his kiss and she wanted so much more.

Ryker pulled his head back and stared down into her eyes. "Cricket, if we don't stop right now, I'm going to carry you up those stairs behind me and make love to you." He watched, so turned on just by the look in her eyes that he was having trouble forming the words. "Do you understand me?" he demanded when she continued to look back up at him with that sultry look in her pretty, green eyes. Damn! He wanted this woman with an almost painful need. He couldn't believe things had gotten so out of hand so quickly. He'd meant to gently kiss her goodnight and then head out. How had it reached the point where he was rock hard and silently begging her to give him permission to continue?

His words slowly broke through her haze of desire and Cricket gasped when she realized the position she was in. "Oh goodness!" she exclaimed and disentangled herself from him.

"Wait! Cricket don't…" and he groaned as her hips shifted against him. Cricket knew exactly what he was dealing with because she felt it too. That crazy, almost painful desire when she moved against his erection shot through her as well. She froze, her body not wanting to do anything that would cause that feeling to happen again. And yet….maybe if she….

"Cricket!" he groaned, closing his eyes and shaking his head. "You know exactly what you're doing, don't you?" he asked, a slight smile on those lips that Cricket now knew could deliver so much pleasure. How could a man that looked this stern and serious know how to kiss like that?

"Sorry," she whispered, her fingers gripping his shoulders so she wouldn't move like that again. "How do I get down without…" she couldn't say the words and knew her face was flaming red now.

"Hold onto me," he told her and moved closer, his hands grabbing onto her hips. With great finesse, he lifted her up and set her down onto the floor once again. "There," he growled, but his hands didn't move away from her and his body pressed against her one more time. "I've got to go," he said with that sexy, husky voice. He didn't leave. His body pressed hers against the door again, his lips finding hers and kissing her again. It was slower this time, sensuous but still got her a little higher on the crazy-for-Ryker scale.

She moaned and her arms moved back up around his neck and she arched into his body, wanting that pleasure back, needing more.

"I have to go," he said again, but his mouth moved against her neck, making her shiver with delight when he found a spot at the base where seemingly all of her nerve endings zipped to attention, sparking that need even higher.

She pulled back slightly, surprised. "You have to go," she whispered, but her fingers remained in his hair and her body was still moving against his

"I'm going to leave now," he said and gritted his teeth. He actually did it this time, pulling back and bracing his arms against the wooden door behind her. "Thank you for tonight," he said and touched her cheek with his rough finger.

She sighed, practically melting against the door behind her. Her fingers were clumsy, barely able to function but she finally was able to find the doorknob. She twisted, didn't get it the first time and tried again. This time, she was able to turn the knob and open the door. She almost forgot to stop leaning against it but, as she practically tripped over her feet when the door pushed her body out of the way, she figured out that she needed to move.

"Goodnight, Cricket," he said again and walked out into the cold night.

Cricket hurried around the room, turning out all the lights as quickly as possible. Then she rushed to the back of her den – just in time to watch him step into his car. When he had the door open and one foot inside, he hesitated and looked back at her house. Cricket stared, biting her lip and praying that he would come back inside and finish what he'd started. She didn't have the courage to ask him herself, but every cell in her body was aching to find out what it would be like to make love with Ryker Thorpe.

In the end, he shook his head and got into the driver's seat. A moment later, his powerful car drove down the street and Cricket sagged against the wall, so disappointed she thought she might actually cry.

Instead, she picked up the two wine glasses and the empty bottle of wine, tossing the bottle into the recycling bin and placing the glasses into the sink before she moved upstairs. Preparing for bed, she drug out her flannel nightgown and pulled it over her head, wishing that she was doing the complete opposite. She actually blushed at all the thoughts that were racing through her mind as she brushed her teeth and washed her face. She didn't really want Ryker to come back. She'd just met the guy today!

She had to remind herself over and over again that this was the kind of man who dined with important people. He wasn't the man for her!

CHAPTER 6

Cricket woke the following morning feeling fresh and alive, and more excited to get to work than she had in a long time. She hurried through her morning routine, eager to get to the office. It had nothing at all to do with her job and everything to do with the idea of seeing Ryker as he walked into the building across the courtyard.

She was ready for her early morning system shock.

Cricket showered and dressed, putting extra effort into her appearance that morning. She even chose a shorter than normal skirt and extra high heels, thinking it wouldn't hurt to be a bit sexier. The man was a genuine hottie, after all.

All her admonishments of the night before were banished from her mind. What harm could come from seeing the man? She was just going to work and, hopefully, he was going to work on his normal schedule. So if they happened to see each other, that didn't mean anything, she told herself. It wasn't a commitment, just an early morning adrenaline rush.

She was grabbing her car keys and purse, checking her lipstick in the mirror one more time when her cell phone rang.

Cricket's whole body cringed and she shook her head when she recognized the ring tone. It wasn't important, she told herself, determined to ignore it. After several rings, it stopped, automatically going to voice mail. When it finally stopped, she took a deep breath and was just about to step out into the crisp, morning air when the ringing started up once more.

She looked at the phone, then shook her head. No one would be calling her at this time of the morning other that those horrible political action calls for surveys. Or it could be her father. Either way, there was no way she was going to answer that call.

Feeling free again, she grabbed her coat, tightening the belt around her waist and rushed out the door. The cool morning air felt fresh and invigorating on her face and she smiled to the sunshine that was just starting to peek over the horizon. Yes, it was going to be a good…

Her phone started ringing again!

"Darn him!" She stopped on her tiny front porch and grabbed the phone out of her purse, flipping it open and answering it with an irritated, "Good morning, Father!"

The answering chuckle only set her nerves on edge.

"Good morning, my beautiful daughter. You're looking exceptionally lovely this fine morning. Is that an excited glow I see on your face or are you just thrilled to hear your old man's voice?"

Cricket looked around, trying to find out where her father was hiding. But she saw nothing and she should have known better. If her father didn't want to be seen, he wouldn't be seen. "Why are you up so early this morning?" she asked, glancing into the trees and the park across the street, anywhere he might be hiding. The man worked nights, was sometimes up all night so how was he still awake this early in the morning?

Her father chuckled softly at her question, obviously enjoying teasing his one and only daughter. "Who says I'm up early? Perhaps I'm up late?"

Her steps froze as she walked to her car and she held her breath as she asked, "You didn't do anything here in Chicago, did you Dad?" She waited several seconds, bracing for his answer. They had an agreement! "You promised," she whispered, anxiety lacing her voice as she waited for him to either confirm or deny whether he had accomplished, or was about to tackle, a project within the metropolitan area of Chicago. He might have agreed to leave this area free of his efforts while she lived here, but that was never a guarantee that he would follow through on his promise.

He was a thief. He obviously had a problem with ethics. She might love him dearly, but she was completely aware of his limitations. If he were tempted by something here in Chicago, a silly promise to his daughter wouldn't stop him.

She walked to her car, unlocking the driver's side door, all the while, looking out the corner of her eye to see if she could spot him somehow.

"I haven't touched a thing in the area in years, my dear. How little faith you have in my promises," he tut-tutted. "But you still haven't answered my question about why you are looking so spiffy. Eager to get to your cold, boring office so you can type in numbers for the rest of the day?" he suggested with the touch of sarcasm that always accompanied his words about her chosen occupation. "Or could that twinkle in your eye have something to do with the man who was in your house last night?" he demanded, his voice no longer as friendly as it was a moment ago.

Cricket was about to start up her car but she stopped, worried now. "You were here last night? You saw…" she had been about to say Ryker's name but stopped herself in time. If her father didn't know who the man was, Cricket wasn't going to give him any hints.

"I know what's going on and you'd better steer clear of Ryker Thorpe," he warned. "The man isn't stupid. He's one of the best lawyers in the country, Cricket. He might not be law enforcement, but don't cross him. He's one of them," he said firmly, saying "them" as if were a four letter word that left a bad taste in his mouth. Her father was very protective, had barely allowed her to date when she'd been younger. No matter where they were in the world, her father had been against her dating. It was only her mother's calming influence that had enabled Cricket to go on dates as a teen. Until she'd gone to college, she'd had very little freedom in the dating area.

Which was ironic. Her mother and father had taught her all these illegal skills, showing her how to break into buildings, steal priceless pieces owned by another human being, but when it came to someone dating his little girl, her father was as protective as a momma bear.

She was shaking her head at this latest invasion of her privacy, wanting to argue with her father, but she couldn't find the words. Possibly because he was right. Ryker was dangerous. She'd found out that Ryker was a lawyer yesterday and it had sent a dangerous thrill throughout her whole body. "If you don't do any jobs in Chicago, there's no reason to be concerned," she pointed out with what she considered irrefutable logic. If the man didn't do anything illegal, he shouldn't be concerned about his daughter dating someone associated with the law.

She could already sense that her father didn't agree. She could feel his anger and frustration coming through the atmosphere to her phone.

"The man's an expert at international law," he stated as if she were being ridiculously stubborn and obtuse. "That means his contacts aren't just in Chicago, Cricket. They're everywhere. The man travels half the year. So not only does that mean he has connections at Interpol, but he wouldn't be good husband material for you. You should be looking for a man who will be home with my grandbabies, helping you raise them. Not off in some foreign country while you stay at home doing diaper duty."

Cricket rolled her eyes. "Dad! I just had a casual night with him. He brought over wine."

There was a long pause before her father finally said, "Cricket, I don't know if you're lying to yourself or to me, but either way, ditch him. He's dangerous."

With those words, he ended the call and Cricket leaned her head against the steering wheel, wishing that her parents were normal and that their chosen career path wasn't so dangerous. And that it didn't interfere with her own life.

She started her car, thinking to ignore his command. She liked Ryker. He was different from the other men she'd either dated or come into contact with over the years. He was kind and sensitive without being wimpy, but also scary smart. And he made her laugh at some of his observations. Even better, he laughed with her! Most men hadn't understood her sense of humor. She knew she was a little off to the left about some things. But Ryker "got" her. Last night, he'd chuckled when she'd told him stories about one thing or another and she'd enjoyed everything about him. Even that scary, almost terrifying attraction she had towards the man.

Goodness, and when he touched her! She'd never experienced anything like that before! She shivered just at the memory and she'd dreamed about him last night in the most erotic, embarrassing way!

Unfortunately, as she drove through the streets of Chicago that were quickly filling up with other commuters, she knew that her father was right. Besides, why waste time enjoying the man's company only to discover that he's a real jerk later on? It would just put her parents in jeopardy. Men always put on a good front initially but once the newness of a relationship wore off, the real person came out. She couldn't risk her parents' future incarceration simply because she thought a man was sexy and funny.

That thought caused another to pop into her head and she used the voice activated phone on her steering wheel to call her father back. When her father picked up, she asked, "Dad, if you're nervous about getting caught, does that mean there's evidence against you?" she asked, suddenly worried.

"Of course not," he growled, his pride in his work wounded. "You know me and your mother better than that." The man considered himself a professional and she had to admit that there hadn't ever been any evidence the police in any country which could connect him to a theft.

So his comments didn't make sense. "So why are you so worried about me seeing a lawyer socially?" she asked, still not convinced.

There was a hesitation on the other end of the line before her father said, "You know that this man is more than a social acquaintance, Cricket. Don't insult me like that."

She shook her head and tried to steer the conversation back to the original subject. "Well, why are you so afraid of this man?"

"Because I don't know everything Interpol has on me or your mother, my dear," he said with strained patience. "They might have our faces, although I doubt it. Or they might know we are connected. You know how it is, Cricket. We've been extremely successful in our careers," he said, that inappropriate pride coming through in his voice once again. "And I doubt your mother or I have made any mistakes, but we're not perfect."

Despite the seriousness of the topic, she had to laugh. "Okay, Dad." She pressed the button on her steering wheel that would disconnect the call and worked her way through the traffic but instead of going straight to the office, which would put her on an intercept course with Ryker at the time they normally walked into the office each morning, she pulled into a coffee shop. Since she couldn't get her daily zing with Ryker's ice blue eyes, she'd treat herself to a special cup of coffee.

Ten minutes later, as she strolled out of the café once again, she knew that the coffee definitely didn't have the same impact on her senses as knowing that Ryker Thorpe was watching her walk into her building. She set her newly acquired and over-priced coffee in the cup holder and meandered her way through traffic to her office, depressed and irritated, the ever present desire to have a normal life creeping up on her.

She couldn't believe how depressed she felt at the idea of not seeing the man. But she told herself over and over that she was being ridiculous. She had spent one night in the man's company. It wasn't like she'd fallen in love with him!

All throughout her childhood, she'd just wanted to be normal, to have friends she knew she could see each day in school. But because of her parents' careers, there were years when she hadn't even been in an official school. Thankfully, her parents pushed her harder than any teacher might. Besides all the skills they'd acquired over the years, they also taught her math, reading and writing. The science part came naturally to her because of all the skills she'd been taught by her parents. She understood chemistry because she'd learned to break into buildings. She had in-depth computer skills because she'd been taught to hack into any computer system or security system.

She sighed and pulled into the parking lot, angry with her parents for such a crazy upbringing. She might have seen the world, but she'd hated every moment of it. When she'd finally gone off to college and formed friendships with her college buddies, she'd thought she'd died and gone to heaven. That had been her first taste at normalcy. Her first freedom from the constant worry about her parents getting caught. It had been wonderful.

And now their chosen occupation was interfering in her life once again. But this felt more harsh than all the other times.

She went through the motions of work, but she didn't really put much effort into it. She might not like her work, but at least before she would take pride in doing the data entry exceptionally well. Today, and for the next three days when she wouldn't allow herself to see Ryker, she thought she genuinely hated her job. If she stared longingly out the window in the hopes of getting a peek at the strong, tall man striding out the office doors towards the parking garage, that certainly couldn't be a crime in her father's world, could it?

It had been bad when she'd had to leave her friends, but for some reason she didn't quite understand, not seeing Ryker every morning felt significantly worse.

By Friday evening, she was exhausted and depressed, feeling angry and resentful at her father for...everything. She walked into her tiny but wonderfully, legally obtained and owned house, dumping her purse and walking straight up the stairs to her bedroom where she flopped backwards onto her bed, staring up at the ceiling.

She didn't even look at the large, glass vase filled to the brim with ball point pens, not wanting to be tempted to get her fix with another early morning nose-snubbing at the expense of her boss. It wouldn't help anyway, she told herself. An adrenaline rush probably wouldn't help her solve her blues this time.

With a sigh, she pulled herself together. Did she really want to jeopardize her parent's security over an exciting fling? She actually hesitated over that answer but realized what she was thinking and shook her head. Of course not! Her parents might be career criminals who just had the luck and intelligence to have not gotten caught, but, except for moving all over the world, they'd been excellent parents. They were kind and caring, giving her experiences other kids couldn't even dream of. So what if she'd been to twenty different countries but her official passport only had two? She knew the languages and, in her mind, she had the memories of all of those adventures. And if it made her stomach churn at the idea of what they did, or the fear of one of them getting caught, it was a small price to pay. They would not be safe with her dating someone as well connected and powerful as Ryker Thorpe.

It wouldn't have worked anyway. Ryker might set her nerve endings on fire with just a touch, but she had to remind herself that he was way out of her league. And besides, what hope did she have of keeping him interested in her long term? She was just an accountant!

She stood up and stripped off her business suit, pulling on a pair of soft, well-worn jeans. One leg had a ragged hem and a back pocket was missing, but these were her favorite jeans, softened by years of washing. Adding a tee-shirt and grabbing a scrunchy to pull her hair off of her neck, she started to feel slightly better. With her work clothes carefully put away, she padded barefoot back downstairs to find something to eat for dinner.

Unfortunately, nothing in her pantry looked appetizing. Her options were limited since she despised going grocery shopping so there wasn't much left. She hadn't been to the grocery store in about two weeks so her choices were a can of tomato soup or a frozen meal, neither of which were particularly appealing.

She probably should have gone out to happy hour with her friends. Unfortunately, she was finding that she didn't have very much to talk about with Josie, Allyson and Debbie. They were wonderful women, but their lives revolved around their kids and their husbands or ex-husbands. It was hard to relate since she was single without kids.

She picked up the can of soup with a grimace. If she'd gone with them, she might have relaxed somewhat or maybe even had something more appetizing to eat than...she opened her freezer and surveyed the stacks of frozen meals...chicken and broccoli. Yuck! Why had she even chosen this one? She hated broccoli!

Then she sighed. Dad! He'd snuck into her house and filled her freezer with healthier choices.

She thought of something else. Closing the freezer, she braced herself to open her fridge and...yep! Filled with fruits and vegetables. She knew they hadn't been there two days ago because she'd grabbed a yogurt yesterday morning for breakfast. But she couldn't guess if he'd filled up her fridge yesterday or today because she'd skipped breakfast this morning and had bought a yogurt at the deli in the building for lunch today.

When the doorbell rang, she actually hoped it was her mother or father. She would love to see them, maybe even cry on their shoulder. Her mother would be better, she thought. At least her mother would understand what she was going through. Her father would just pat her shoulder and tell her that Ryker wasn't the man for her. That she should get over him and find a nice, reliable, non-lawyerly type of man to fall in love with and give him grandchildren.

Tossing the frozen meal back into the freezer, she almost skipped to the front door.

Just as she was opening the door, suddenly realizing that she hadn't looked through her peep hole to see who was there, it occurred to her that her parents wouldn't ring the doorbell. They wouldn't even knock. In fact, if it were her parents, they would be sitting in her den, reading the newspaper or a book.

By the time all those thoughts raced through her mind, the door was open and she was staring at a very handsome, very tall and very muscular Ryker Thorpe.

"You've been avoiding me," he said as he stepped into her miniscule foyer. "And you didn't call me." He stepped closer to her, taking the door out of her hand and slamming it shut behind him. "So I stopped waiting," he said and took her into his arms.

Cricket was stiff for perhaps one, maybe two seconds before the heat of his arms and the deliberate, commanding feel of his lips snapped her out of it and she was curling into his embrace, kissing him back with all the feeling she'd denied herself by not seeing him each morning. Her arms wrapped around his neck and her body plastered against his, feeling all those delicious hard planes that were so completely different from her body and sent breathtaking zings all throughout her system.

When he deepened the kiss, she heard herself whimper, but couldn't stop her arms from reaching up and wrapping around his neck, her leg shifting so his…was that…? Yes, she pressed her tummy closer, feeling his erection against her belly and her whole body melted even more. She felt the wall behind her back and was relieved, using it to press herself more fully against him, stretching up on her toes to feel him in more places. When she felt his hand under her sweater, she almost sobbed out with the excitement that she couldn't control. And didn't want to.

She'd never felt anything like this before and she didn't want it to stop. This was ten times better than sneaking through some security system! No adrenaline rush could make her feel this…exhilarated!

Cricket felt her body lifted, her back pressing harder against the wall and she instinctively lifted her legs, wrapping them around his waist while his body pressed against her own. She felt his hands underneath her shirt and gasped at the contact, her eyes opening wide to look into his. Slowly, ever so slowly, his hand moved against her bare skin. Cricket wasn't aware of her mouth falling open, or her eyes almost closing while her hips shifted along with his hand.

She heard him growl for some reason, but all she cared about was his hands on her skin, wanting more. Needing more! "Please don't stop," she begged when his hands moved away from her skin.

"I don't intend to," he growled right back, lifting her higher into his arms.

Cricket had no idea what was happening, only that he'd moved her hips so she wasn't feeling that delicious pressure anymore and she squirmed in his arms, trying to bring back that feeling, to appease the ache that was building in her body.

"Ryker! You're not…"

"I will be," he came back, his voice still barely above a growl.

She sighed with happiness when she felt the softness at her back but she couldn't stop touching him long enough to realize that it was her bed. She didn't care that he'd brought her up to her bedroom, not even sure how he'd accomplished something so effortlessly. All she cared about was feeling his strong fingers against her skin again. She took his hand and placed it against her stomach, then moved her own hands up to the buttons on his shirt, almost ripping the buttons open in her desperate need to discover what lay beneath those expensive shirts.

She wasn't disappointed, her fingers roaming over his heated skin, feeling his muscles flinch wherever she touched. She was so fascinated, that she lifted her head, her tongue darting out to taste that amazing skin and all the enthralling muscles that flexed and shifted under her fingers.

Cricket was only vaguely aware of Ryker pulling her sweater over her head and tossing it somewhere. She didn't want to think any longer. It had been a week of worrying and denial but she couldn't deny herself anything any longer. She'd wanted this man three nights ago. She'd denied herself then and every morning after. No more!

She arched against him, whimpering when he pulled her white, lace bra off of her shoulder so he could kiss the peak of her breast. Her leg rose up, pressing against his thigh and her hips pressed, seeking that special pressure she'd discovered the last time he'd been here. She wanted it, needed it!

"Please!" she begged him when he moved his mouth away from her breast but just about sighed with happiness when he pulled the strap down on the other side, taking her nipple in his mouth and sucking. Then it wasn't a sigh. She screamed out with the new feelings that jolted her. She pressed her hips against him harder, still trying to find that special place on his body that felt so perfect.

His mouth moved lower and she felt his fingers expertly open the button on her jeans. A moment later, her jeans were gone along with her white, lace underwear. She was completely naked underneath him but she needed to touch him as well. He was too far down her body now for her to do anything. When his mouth kissed her stomach, she wiggled, smiling as he tickled her.

When his mouth found that special place, she just about screamed again. But his arm was heavy over her hips, holding her down. She had no intention of pulling away but she couldn't deal with that kind of pleasure. It was so powerful and then he started sucking, one finger moving inside of her and she simply couldn't hold back any longer. That ache that had been building to unbearable heights exploded. Her whole body exploded. She closed her eyes as she screamed out, her climax shooting waves of intense pleasure throughout her whole being.

And when it was over, she lay on the bed, panting with her eyes closed, not sure how to even open them and look at him after that kind of experience.

Ryker stood up and tore his clothes off. When he was finally naked, he looked down at the woman on her bed, surrounded by flowered sheets and flowered pillows and still reeling in the haze of her climax. Damn, he'd never been this impatient before. He felt like a teenager again but he couldn't deny that Cricket was the sexiest, most sensuous woman he'd ever seen. Tasting her orgasm had made him almost lose control. The only thing that held him back was the incredible pleasure of seeing her fall apart at his touch.

He pulled the condom out of his wallet, and put it on, all the while watching as she slid against the sheets in the aftermath of her climax. Bending lower, he nuzzled her neck, finding that magic spot on her neck he'd discovered only moments ago. Sure enough, she gasped and reacted instantly. Her arms moved to his shoulders, a little slower this time, but when his fingers slid inside of her, he knew that she was right back with him.

"Hold onto me, Cricket," he said and lifted her arms so they were around his neck once again. "Look at me," he said and moved her legs wider so they could accommodate his hips. With the slightest movement, he slid inside her just an inch. When her eyes widened, he moved a bit deeper. Inch by inch, he pressed into her heat, then out again, watching her face for signs that he was doing something she liked or didn't like. He felt the sweat break out on his back and forehead as he worked hard to keep control. He wanted this first time with her to be incredible, but it was using everything inside of him to slow down, to make sure she was enjoying this as much as he was. But as her tight heat gripped him, he pressed deeper.

When he saw the flinch on her face and her eyes closed briefly, he stopped and looked down at her. "Cricket?" he asked. "Are you okay?"

She wiggled her hips slightly, trying to get used to his size. Biting her lip, she shifted again, not seeing the almost pained look in his eyes until she opened her own again and looked up at him. When she saw what was going on with him, her hand moved to his cheek. "What's wrong?" she whispered, worried that she'd done something wrong. "Did I hurt you?" she asked.

"Damn no!" he groaned. "But I think I just hurt you," he said. He tried not to move, suspecting that this was her first time; he didn't want her to be hurt any more than was needed. He cursed himself for moving so fast. He should have been more patient. He should have gotten to know her better. If he had gone slower, if he'd just talked to her like he'd planned tonight, then he might have known that she was a virgin. Or had been.

"I'm sorry, Cricket," he growled, berating himself for being so obtuse. "I didn't know."

She moved her hips again, the pain completely gone and the need to move, to feel him inside of her was more overpowering than she could have imagined. "I'm good," she said, then gasped when he moved just slightly.

"Are you sure?" he asked, freezing once again.

She wiggled her hips and placed her hands on his chest, the need to move becoming more urgent. "Ryker, please don't stop," she gasped out and then closed her eyes once again when he did just that, shifting his weight which caused him to shift inside of her, delicious, amazing and overwhelming pleasure zipped through her whole body and she closed her eyes, arching into him to feel it again.

That was all the encouragement he needed. Ryker pulled slightly out of her heat, then pressed right back into her. Over and over again, faster and faster, he watched her climb up that pleasure cliff with him and it was such a turn-on to see her like this, to know that he was the only man who had done this to her. When she screamed out with her second orgasm, the tightness of her brought him right along with her. He'd wanted to watch her, but the way she writhed underneath him pulled him over to his own climax.

Cricket felt like she was showered in waves of pleasure so intense, she saw spots and lights and stars. When it was all over, she fell back against her quilt, feeling boneless. She felt him move, but she couldn't figure out why or what he might be doing. He came back from the bathroom and curled up behind her, pulling her close while he kissed her shoulder and neck.

She sighed with happiness as Ryker's fingers skimmed along her hip, tickling her waist. She laughed when he started to move higher, grabbing his fingers and looked over her shoulder at him. He was propped up on his elbow, looking down at her and she blushed at the look in his eyes.

"You think that's going to stop me?" he asked, his hand moving around to her stomach and pulling her more tightly against his chest, her bottom snuggled against his groin.

"No," she smiled and wiggled her derriere.

She felt a sharp sting when his hand smacked her bottom lightly. It wasn't hard enough to hurt, but it was surprising and she looked over her shoulder at him inquiringly.

"You're trying to tempt me into doing everything once more but I need nourishment if you want to ravish me again."

She laughed happily, but her body was tingling from that touch and the look in his eyes. "I think we need to determine who ravished whom tonight," she said, feeling cold when he stood up from her bed. She pulled the soft comforter over her nakedness, but fully admired his own muscular body as he walked into her bathroom.

"I have frozen dinners in the freezer if you're hungry," she said, pushing the pillows behind her so she could sit up and have a better view.

He came back into her bedroom, amused with her modesty. "I actually brought Chinese food with me," he said.

She was surprised. And tempted! "You did?" she asked. "Where is it?"

Ryker put his hands on his hips and shook his head, apparently just as confused as she was. "I believe it's still on your foyer floor. I think I dropped it when you attacked me as I entered your house a few hours ago."

"I attacked you?" she gasped, holding the blanket over her breasts but her hunger suddenly resurfaced. Then she leaned back against her pillow again, a twinkle entering her eyes. "I hope my dog didn't eat the food," she teased.

Ryker froze and looked back at her, surprised. "You have a dog?" He was immediately moving towards the door and stairs but he glanced back, saw the mischief in her eyes and stopped.

Cricket couldn't stop the laughter at his surprised, confused expression. "No. But I had you fooled for a moment, didn't I?"

Ryker wasn't going to take that. He might have chuckled, but he also stormed right back to her bed and pulled the blanket off of her. "You're going to pay for that," he said a moment before his hand grabbed her ankle as she tried to laughingly get away from him. It was no contest and a moment later, she was right back in his arms, his mouth covering hers and that now familiar but still shocking tidal wave of desire came over her, swamping her senses. She lifted her arms, wrapping them around his neck as she gave in to the storm.

Another hour and an invigorating shower later, and they were sitting at her kitchen table eating re-heated Chinese food directly out of the containers, arguing about one thing after another. She pushed the chicken and broccoli away from her, wrinkling her nose when he stabbed a broccoli stalk and offered it to her. He laughed and caught her foot with both of his as she tried to push his chair farther away.

"So you don't like broccoli," he said and popped the vegetable into his mouth with a wink in her direction. "And you've never had sex before today. You're still embarrassed to be naked around me," he teased as he snuck a peek down the loose neck of the robe she'd pulled on after their shower, "and you don't have a dog. What else don't I know about you?" he asked.

Cricket thought about her parents but then pushed them out of her mind. Ryker didn't want to know her whole history. "I hate grocery stores, I hate to cook and I'm afraid of spiders. What more do you want to know?"

He pulled her onto his lap and wrapped his arms around her, feeding himself from behind her while she rested her back against his chest, feeding herself except for the times when he stole whatever chunk she was about to eat herself. All the while, they talked about themselves, learning all those things that should have been discussed before they'd had sex. It was sweet and wonderful, even if Cricket sometimes worried that her father might be outside watching her.

And when they'd filled themselves with Chinese food, he picked her up into his arms and carried her back to her bedroom to make love to her throughout the night.

A long time later, when they were snuggled underneath her flowered quilt and their bodies barely able to move any more, she heard him say, "Come to Paris with me."

She'd been half asleep but had woken when he had a moment ago although she still felt like snuggling into her pillow with him curled up behind her. She opened one eye, trying to determine if he was serious. The look in those blue eyes told her that he was completely serious and she rolled over, completely awake now. "I can't go to Paris with you," she answered, surprised but feeling wonderful that he'd asked.

Ryker shifted their positions so she was underneath him. "Of course you can. Just call your boss and tell him you need some personal days," he said, kissing her shoulder, her arm. When his mouth took her finger and started sucking, the jolt went straight to her core and she gasped.

"No Paris," she struggled to say, all the while shifting her body underneath his better so she could get what she wanted, which was him, inside her and moving in that magical way that destroyed her control and made her feel like she was floating among the stars.

"Why not?" he asked, sliding into her heat and watching her face, his body actually becoming harder when her mouth fell open and her eyes closed, sheer bliss on her beautiful, makeup free face. Her blond curls were spread out on the pillow and her body was gorgeously naked and moving against his instinctively. Ryker could honestly say that he'd never had a more incredibly sexual experience with another woman. And he didn't want it to stop despite the fact that he had an important meeting in Paris the next day. "It will be for just three days and we can be together."

"Sounds perfect," she replied, her hands clenching his shoulders. "But if you could just…concentrate on the here and now," she said, lifting her hips, silently begging him to move faster, press deeper.

After hours of making love to this woman, he knew exactly what she wanted but he didn't give it to her. He held back even though his own body was clamoring for him to give in and just enjoy the incredible feel of her, he wanted this to go on longer. Forever possibly.

"Agree to come to Paris then."

Cricket was ready to scream, needing him to just… "Paris is too far away."

"I can get you there in six hours," he said, shifting just the way she liked him to move.

"Can't!" she groaned and moved herself, knowing that he liked that…yep, just like that, she smiled when he groaned himself.

"You can," he whispered back.

In response, she moved her hand down his back, her fingers trailing against his skin and she almost laughed out loud when she won the argument and he gave both of them what they desperately needed.

CHAPTER 7

Cricket smiled as she let herself into her house, thinking about Ryker's request this morning for her to travel with him to Paris. What a romantic!

It was quiet now that he was gone and she lugged her groceries into the kitchen. She knew her father had stocked her fridge, but he hadn't loaded it with appropriate levels of carbs and fats. She'd bought ice cream and potato chips along with some chicken breasts and a few things that would make a good dinner. In her mind, she was planning a romantic meal with Ryker when he returned from Paris in three days. He said he would call and let her know when he was landing and she'd loved the way he'd said goodbye to her this morning.

"Wipe that silly smile off of your face!"

Cricket yelped and jumped at least a foot in the air, dropping both bags of groceries onto the floor which then scattered their contents everywhere, including the ice cream which exploded in every direction on impact.

Cricket looked at the mess, then glanced up, her face still shocked. "Dad! What are you doing in my house!" she exclaimed angrily.

Her father was one of those extremely handsome, dangerously charming and irritatingly good thieves. To date, there wasn't a lock he couldn't pick or a safe he couldn't open. In his mind, security systems were more of an amusement to him than a hindrance.

"Do I need an excuse to come visit my favorite daughter?" he joked.

Cricket wasn't in the mood to be teased. "I'm your only daughter! And yes, you should wait for an invitation before letting yourself in." She grabbed the broom and started sweeping up the spilled cereal and broken cookies. "Did you at least use the key I gave you or did you pick my lock?"

"Of course I didn't use a key!" he scoffed. He stood there while she swept up the mess, shaking his head as if he were shocked by her groceries. "Why did you even need to go shopping? I bought you everything you need just the other day."

She dumped the first load into the trashcan. "You know I don't like broccoli, Dad," she said and picked up what remained of her ice cream, sighing when she accepted that it was a total loss before dumping it too into the trash can. "Why couldn't you have let me know you were here at least?"

He crossed his arms over his chest, glaring at her with admonishment. "I didn't want to run into anyone I wasn't supposed to run into."

Cricket looked up at him, suddenly wary. "About that," she started to say.

"You're still seeing him!" her father roared, throwing his arms up in the air with profound exasperation. "Even after I told you to stop seeing him, he was in this house, wasn't he?"

Cricket refused to be intimidated by her father's anger. This was her house and he had no business trying to tell her who could and couldn't come into her own home. "How do you know I'm still seeing him?" she yelled right back at him, undaunted since she knew that his bark was much worse than his bite. The man was a pussy cat, actually. Some people might be frightened of him, but she knew he wouldn't hurt her in any way. Except to drive her crazy sometimes. And continue in a career that scared the bejeezus out of her for fear of losing him to prison.

"Are you kidding me?" he demanded, standing over her and trying to make her feel his wrath. "The man was here all last night! He even came downstairs with…"

"Don't say it!" she told him, covering his mouth with her open palm. "Don't you dare say it because then I'll know you were spying on me last night and I would consider that a huge violation of the trust I thought we shared together."

Edward Fairchild grabbed her wrist and pulled her hand away from his mouth. "All trust issues are null and void when you start sleeping with the enemy," he told her.

She couldn't believe he was saying things like that! "Ryker Thorpe is not the enemy. He is a very nice man."

Edward waited for her to continue, but when she hesitated, he rolled his eyes. "Do not tell me that you're falling in love with a lawyer. You know what that would do to your mother!"

Cricket pulled back, horrified at what might happen. "What's wrong with Mom?" she asked, instantly worried.

Her father continued to glower at her, but seeing the worry in her eyes, he relented slightly. "Nothing. Yet. But if she found out that you were sleeping around, she'd be very, very upset!"

Cricket swallowed painfully, trying not to let her father know how much that hurt. "Is Mom here?" she asked, hiding her face from his view.

Edward stared down at the back of his daughter's head, knowing she was close to tears. "She's in Rome right now, shopping I think."

Cricket's whole body froze and she looked up at her father, anxiety showing in the green depths. "Shopping-shopping? Or shopping for something…in particular that might not be…"

"She's just spending money, honey. Nothing nefarious." He pushed away from the counter and took her hands, lifting her up and giving her a gentle hug. "Don't worry about your Momma," he told her softly. "But don't put her in jeopardy by continuing to see this man. He's bad news. I can feel it in my bones."

Cricket felt like her heart was breaking. She wanted so desperately to tell her father that she would continue to see Ryker. She wanted him to understand that the man made her feel special and pretty, feminine. And the way he touched her! She'd never felt anything like this with another man. Even beyond the physical side of their relationship, she loved just talking to him.

But how could she be happy when that very happiness put her parents in danger? "He's a very nice man, Dad," she said with hope that he would understand.

His face was implacable. "He's part of the system. We've already had this conversation."

"You could stop stealing stuff," she offered hopefully. "Then it wouldn't be a problem for me to see Ryker." She would love it if her parents would change their occupation, or even just retire! What would be the harm in them stopping their projects?

Her dad pulled back and shook his head. "Gotta go, my love. I'll see you soon, okay?"

Cricket watched with growing resentment as her father walked out of her house. At least he unlocked the door this time. That was something. That's what she told herself anyway but it didn't soothe her aching heart at the thought of not seeing Ryker again.

She bent down to clean up the rest of the trashed groceries from the floor, salvaging what she could. And then, because she was so depressed about her father's demands, she took the saved box of Oreo cookies, plunked herself down in her favorite chair and ate cookies for lunch, ignoring all the healthy fruit and vegetables he'd provided for her. It was a petty, childish backlash, but it made her feel somewhat in control of her life.

When a whole line of Oreos were gone and she still didn't feel better, she knew there was only one thing she could do. It would help her get out of her doldrums and would clear her mind. With a smile of anticipation, she hurried up the stairs to her room and pulled on her "going out" clothes, then her jeans and sweatshirt over top of that. It was a cool evening and it would be an even colder night. Perfect for going out.

This was one reason she didn't condemn her parents so completely for their lifestyle. She knew the thrill of success and the excitement of planning. She stopped at the hardware store and got all of the equipment she would need, then hit the dollar store to get wrapping paper. The cashier looked at her somewhat strangely when she came up to the cash register with twenty rolls of various wrapping paper, but when she said, "It's a surprise for my boss," the cashier just smiled and rung up the various items.

She ran from store to store, gathering the other items she would need, careful to only spend cash and also to not buy too much in one place. The dollar store was the only exception and she knew that would be okay since people bought strange things from that place all the time for projects and parties and such.

She was humming as she strolled down the street, feeling like a normal person and hoping she looked like one. But inside, her mind was going through all the minute details, anticipating whatever new security Jason might have installed and going over the information she knew about the security guards' routines. She almost giggled out loud in anticipation!

It was finally dark enough for her exploration. She worked her way up the building, coming in from a different route this time. She looked around, her eyes surveying the equipment in place. There was a heat sensor installed now. That was pretty good, she thought. Heat sensors were very difficult to even perceive, much less circumvent, since their alarm was triggered when the heat in the room rose in any way. Normally, they were set to adjust for the thermostat's inability to keep the area at a constant temperature.

With shining eyes, she disabled the sensor and patched in a software program that would keep the alarm system from realizing that the sensors were down. Scooting forward, she disabled two more issues, and then looked around for any other issues.

When she felt safe enough, she went to work. It took her over an hour to accomplish everything but by the time she was slithering out, again on a different route from her entrance, and re-enabling all of the security systems, she felt enormously better.

CHAPTER 8

Cricket sighed as she got out of her car several days later. She wouldn't see Ryker today even though she knew he'd returned from Paris yesterday afternoon. He'd left her a message on her cell phone letting her know and asking her to meeting him for dinner.

She hadn't returned his phone call and this morning she was completely off schedule in order to avoid running into him. She should be brave and just call him back, explain that she couldn't see him anymore. But she knew what would happen when she heard his voice. She'd completely cave in and try to figure out a way to be with him without her father knowing.

It was pointless, she told herself. She needed to be firm, mostly with her own mind and body, both of which were craving just the sight of him. She'd love to curl up in his arms and feel those wonderful, tingling sensations that only he could give her. But she had to stay away from him.

Now if she could just stop thinking about him!

Rounding the corner to her office, she had come in the back way just to guarantee that she wouldn't....

She gasped as someone grabbed her arm and pulled her into one of the lobby hallways. She was just about to fight, her natural instincts rising up, when she realized that it was Ryker's hand and Ryker's body that was pressing her against the wall. And then she sighed with happiness when Ryker's mouth descended to hers and smothered whatever protest she was going to make. She kissed him back with all the emotions she'd been bottling up inside of her, eager to taste and feel him once again.

He lifted his head briefly to look down at her and she smiled up at him. "You're back!" she sighed, shifting her body against his and wishing desperately that it was still summer and she wasn't wearing this bulky coat. "I can't see you," she whispered, but her head tilted back, begging him to kiss her.

He must have felt the same way since his fingers moved away from her waist and deftly unbuttoned her coat, slipping his body closer and Cricket sighed with desire as she felt more of his hard angles and planes. "You feel wonderful," she whispered, her fingers clenching at his shoulders as if he might get away from her.

"Why didn't you call me back?" he said while his head dipped lower to kiss her neck.

She tilted her head to the side, enjoying the frizzle of excitement that shot down her body. "Because," was all she would say for an explanation. In her mind, she was trying to come up with a solution that would work with her father, but when he was touching her in this way, she wasn't able to think about anything other than his touch.

He bit her neck hard enough to make her gasp and jerk away, but not hard enough to hurt. "Give me a better reason," he growled in her ear.

"Because I can't see you," she said with a groan while her hands smoothed down his body from his shoulders to his stomach, teasing him in the same way he was doing to her on her neck.

He grabbed her hands before they could move any lower. "That's not really an explanation. Nor is it even going to work. We will be seeing each other."

She sighed and laid her head against the wall behind her. "We can't."

He chuckled. "You're going to have to give me a better explanation than that," he said and pressed his knee between her legs, causing her whole body to jerk in reaction. Her eyes closed. He pressed her hips against his leg, shifting ever so slightly until he caught her shudder in his arms. "What's going on Cricket?" he asked, holding her hips so she couldn't move away from him.

She bit her lip, trying to control her body's reaction but it was pointless. They'd spent only one night together but he already knew her body well enough, knew what she wanted and how to make her body hum with need.

"You're not playing fair," she whispered through clenched teeth.

"I don't ever play fair. Tell me what's going on."

"My father doesn't want us seeing each other."

His hands moved higher along the silk of her blouse, easily finding her nipples underneath the smooth material. His thumb was merciless as he flicked the peak to hardness. She tried to grab his hands and pull them away, but she was his sexual prisoner for the moment. "Your father can't control us, Cricket. You're an adult."

"You don't understand," she said, begging him with her eyes to stop torturing her like this.

Ryker sighed with frustration and need. He hadn't planned on seducing her in the hallway of her office building so he'd completely messed this up. But she hadn't called and she hadn't arrived at work at her normal time so he'd been frustrated and determined to know what had happened in the past three days. It hadn't ever occurred to him that her parents would interfere.

Unfortunately, he had a meeting and he knew she had to get to work. "Meet me for dinner tonight and we'll discuss it," he said, shifting his leg ever so slightly in the hopes that she would agree.

"I can't," she argued, but her body shifted again.

Ryker knew exactly what she was doing and if sex was the only way he could get to her, he'd use it. He wanted this woman, but he wanted more than just sex. He pulled his leg away and almost laughed with the frustrated look on her face. "Meet me for dinner and we'll continue this afterwards," he coaxed, bending down and going straight for that spot on her neck.

Cricket whimpered, her hands both holding him in place one moment, then wanting to push him away. Her fingers gripped his hair, unsure of which need was more overpowering, the one to make him stop or the one to make him finish what he'd started.

"I can't."

His fingers moved up to cup her breast once again, his thumb hovering over her nipple. "Just dinner, Cricket. No harm in meeting me for dinner."

Cricket held her breath, her whole body primed to feel his thumb on her nipple. But he didn't touch her, just hovered, driving her crazier than she'd ever thought possible.

"Dinner. Fine!" she screamed and was rewarded by his thumb flicking over her nipple again. It was both sweet and painful since there was no way to culminate this liaison and her need for him was making her crazy.

Ryker stepped back, his eyes hot with his own need shining through. "I'll pick you up," he said.

"No!" she gasped, not wanting her father to see Ryker arrive. "I'll meet you somewhere," she countered. "Just give me an address."

Ryker didn't like that suggestion. He wanted to pick her up and talk to her in the privacy of her house where they wouldn't be disturbed. He fully intended to take her out for dinner, but he wanted answers first. He could see in her eyes that she wasn't going to give in on this issue so he relented, wanting her company too much to argue. "Fine. Meet me at Simpson's at seven. Does that work for you?" he asked gently, wanting to grab her back into his arms and find a more private place to finish what he'd started, but that was impossible.

"Simpson's," she repeated and nodded her head to reinforce it. "Yes. Seven o'clock, I'll be there."

He watched her closely, seeing something in her eyes that worried him. "If you're not there, Cricket, I'll come to your house and wait until you arrive. I'm not giving up on you. And whatever is going on, we'll work through it."

She nodded numbly, but brushed past him as she hurried back to the main lobby area. She pressed the elevator call button with shaking fingers, eager to get up to her office and pull herself together again. Good grief, the man knew what he was doing!

Once she had the door to her office closed behind her, she took several deep breaths. Running her hand over the stacks of invoices and reports, she grounded herself in reality. Ryker was fantasy. This was real. This was what was important. Normalcy. Her parents. Ryker was a fling that could destroy her family. Her job and her parents, they would be with her forever.

Yes, she told herself firmly as she turned on her computer and logged into her e-mails, this was what she should be focusing on. She shouldn't have let him kiss her. She shouldn't have even spoken to him. If he did that again, she'd just press her hand against his chest to keep him away.

The image of his broad, muscular chest came to mind. And all the ways she'd touched that chest a few nights ago. He tasted so good. And he had that sexy indentation right under his breast plate. She'd run her finger over that place several times, fascinated with the area. He'd even shuddered when she'd kissed his flat nipples. She smiled at the memory and her body reacted.

"Who is he?" Josie asked, leaning against the door to her office.

Cricket jumped about a foot in the air, almost falling off of her chair at Josie's voice. She'd thought she was alone!

"Who's who?" she asked, grabbing onto the chair and pulling herself back into place. She smoothed her hair and laid her hands over the papers on her desk.

"Who is the guy you're thinking about?" she clarified, her eyes excited at the prospect.

"Is Jason in? Shouldn't we be working?" she asked.

"Jason is out of town this week so we have a quiet few days ahead of us," she explained with relish. She moved away from the doorway and came to sit down in her chair. "So spill it. Who's the guy?"

Cricket shrugged. "What guy?"

Josie laughed and shook her head. "The fact that you keep repeating that phrase only makes me more positive that you have a new guy in your life. So who is he?" she demanded. "Come on, give us a hint. I've been married for fifteen years and I have four kids. I have to live through your escapades and this is the first time I've heard of you doing anything other than working. So tell me!" she teased.

Cricket shook her head. "I'm not seeing anyone," she told Josie. And it was only partially a lie. She wasn't supposed to be seeing Ryker. And just because she'd agreed to meet him for dinner, that didn't mean she actually would get to the restaurant.

Besides, had she really seen him this morning? Only briefly, which technically counted, she guessed. But most of the time her eyes had been closed so she didn't feel like she was genuinely lying to her friend.

"If it wasn't a guy, what put that dreamy, star gazing look on your face?" she asked, not believing Cricket for a moment.

Cricket felt the blush coming up her neck and tried to stop it, but since she'd never felt this way about a man, she'd had no idea if it was even possible.

"You are! You're seeing someone!" she laughed, pointing at Cricket's now-pink cheeks. "Who is he?" she demanded, on the edge of her chair now. "Is he someone in this building?"

"No!" Cricket exclaimed, worried that Josie would follow her around and find out the truth. "Seriously, I'm not dating anyone." She made the assertion with a strong voice and prayed that Josie would believe her this time. She couldn't imagine how embarrassing it would be if anyone caught her doing what she and Ryker had been doing earlier this morning.

Josie clapped her hands excitedly. "Is he hot? Is he absolutely gorgeous? Or is he one of those geeky, cerebral types that make one think of dark, desperate poetry?"

Cricket stared at Josie for a long, pregnant moment before the woman's words sunk in. She laughed and leaned back in her chair, wondering how Josie ever came up with these ideas. "Josie, you read way too many romance novels."

"I know. Now stop changing the subject and tell me what he does for a living. Is he rich?" Her eyes narrowed as she watched for any reaction on Cricket's face. "No, he's probably one of those desperately poor men who are more earthy and yummy."

"Why do you think that?" she couldn't help but ask.

Josie grinned and bounced a little in her chair. "Because you're one of those extremely nice women who don't hurt any sort of living thing. So it would be natural for you to be attracted to someone who needs your sort of compassion and understanding."

Cricket blinked, wondering where Josie had gotten the idea that she was a nice person. She hadn't ever thought about that before, always striving just to be perceived as normal. "You think I'm nice?" she asked, feeling a startling sense of warmth seep through her body at the idea. She also had to laugh at the idea of Ryker Thorpe needing anyone's compassion or understanding. She didn't know him very well, but what she did know of him, she could tell that he wasn't the kind of man who would need anyone, much less their compassion. And understanding? He went his own way, forging his own path. People came to him for his understanding, not the other way around.

"Of course you're nice," Josie replied, rolling her eyes. "Probably too nice which is why you need to 'fess up and let me stalk your man for a little while, find out if he's good enough for you. I wouldn't want some creepy guy trying to spin you up into a frazzle and then dump you later on."

Cricket thought about Ryker's hands and mouth this morning. Yes, he'd definitely worked her up into a "frazzle" this morning. She blinked and refocused on Josie, shaking her head at the ridiculous thoughts she was having about Ryker. "I'm fine. And I'm just as boring as I was yesterday and the day before." That was a perfectly honest statement if she'd ever heard one. "And there's no guy in my life. I have a very obnoxious father who steps in whenever he thinks I'm dating someone so it's too hard right now. Maybe later," she told Josie, feeling her heart clench at the idea of never seeing Ryker again. But that was how it had to be.

Cricket's phone rang at that moment and their work day started. Just because their boss was out of the office didn't mean there wasn't work to be done. Cricket worked through the stacks of invoices on her desk, diligently ensuring they were all accurate and in the system to be paid. When she finished that stack, she pulled the second one forward, refusing to give in to the feeling of being a gerbil running around on an exercise wheel but never making any progress. This was what she wanted, she told herself. There wasn't anything more normal than accounting.

As she worked through her tasks that afternoon, her mind was frantically working out what she was going to do about dinner tonight. She'd told him that she was going to meet him, but that had been this morning. At that point, she'd had every intention of calling him up and canceling, then figuring out how to be away from her house so he couldn't find her there either. It was a cowardly instinct, but she hadn't figured out a better plan.

She sat in her office, contemplating her options. What she should do was just send him a message telling him that she wouldn't be able to meet him for dinner. No explanations, no apologies. She should simply break off all communications with him.

But she knew that she couldn't just leave him hanging like that. He deserved better treatment than that. She wasn't just attracted to him like crazy now. She respected him. She'd listened to him while they'd conversed and she suspected that he really was a brilliant, powerful lawyer and a good man. Those didn't come around very often.

It took her forty-five minutes to reach the restaurant, but only because she had to go around and backtrack. She suspected that she saw her father at one point, but she wasn't certain. By the time she arrived at the restaurant, she was flustered from walking so much and she was later than she'd anticipated. She stopped in the lobby, hurriedly slipping her running shoes off and putting her heels back on so Ryker wouldn't notice that she'd walked most of the way. She suspected that he would be furious with her about that and she didn't want to argue with him.

She was just turning around to speak to the hostess when Ryker stepped forward. One eyebrow was raised as he watched her shove her running shoes into her black bag.

"I just needed some exercise," she told him.

Ryker's eyebrow actually went a little higher and she bit her lip, hoping he wouldn't question her explanation. Because it didn't really make a lot of sense. Especially since he could have driven both of them, or she could have. They were right across the courtyard from each other.

No, this wasn't going to work, she told herself as she followed Ryker and the hostess to their table. When the waiter had taken their orders and disappeared once again, Cricket leaned back in her chair, knowing she had to end this but not sure how. She was becoming a yoyo, she thought miserably. One moment, she wanted to jump into his arms, the next moment she was so flustered at the idea of her father catching them, she was trying to figure out how to end the relationship that had barely started. She was a mess! She'd never been this pathetic before! Her father was driving her nuts!

She took a deep breath, ready to start the discussion but at the same moment, the wine steward arrived with the wine Ryker had ordered. She snapped her mouth shut and waited as patiently as possible while he went through the whole wine pouring process. When he was gone and they were once again alone, she took a long sip of the excellent wine. When she set it down again, he was already waiting for her, obviously knowing she had something to discuss.

"We can't see each other anymore," she finally said and then closed her eyes at how horrible that statement came out. She opened them again, trying to gauge his reaction. Oddly, he didn't look upset or irritated.

"Why is that?" he asked, leaning forward and looking at her across the linen covered tablecloth. The candlelight made his face look more angular, but softened those angles at the same time. Even his ice blue eyes looked lighter somehow.

Cricket tried to come up with a reason that would make sense, but how does one tell a magnificent, sexy, confident man that her father wouldn't approve of him? In Ryker's case, the idea was ludicrous.

"It's complicated," she finally blurted out.

"So un-complicate it and give me your reasons." He took a sip of wine. "It obviously isn't that we're not attracted to each other."

She flushed red with that comment since he was right. It was very hard for her to deny that she was attracted to him when she couldn't seem to stay out of his arms.

And every time he held her, she was ravenous for him. "No. I think you're right about that being obvious."

"So what's the problem?"

Cricket held her wine glass as if it were a lifesaver. "I don't really have a traditional background," she said, knowing that wasn't enough of an explanation, but she wasn't sure what to say next without revealing something that would put him in an awkward situation and her parents in prison.

"Tell me about it," he encouraged patiently. When she still hesitated, he started to tell her stories about growing up as the oldest of four boys. Cricket was so captivated by his stories, she forgot to get him to understand why she couldn't see him any longer.

"So when your parents died, all of your brothers were already in college?" she asked, fascinated.

"Yes. At various levels and all over the country."

"And you flew out to each of them to tell them the news in person." She'd already figured that out from some of the other things he'd said.

"Yes. And brought them all back for the funeral."

"That must have been hard since they were in the four corners of the country. How did you do it in time?"

Ryker smiled slightly. "Despite our growing years and the antics the three younger ones got into during high school, they're all pretty responsible."

"So they just got on the plane with you and came back?"

"Basically, yes."

She nodded her head, more impressed with him every time she spoke to him. "And you were dealing with your own grief the whole time."

"Getting my brothers back home helped a lot."

"And now you all work together. How did the four of you end up becoming lawyers?"

He smiled, remembering some of the arguments in their household about the subject. "We might all be lawyers, but we specialize in different kinds of law. For instance, Xander does family law, which basically translates into him being a damn fine divorce attorney."

She cringed, thinking of what kind of an impact that would have psychologically on a single man. "So he sees the worst in most relationships, doesn't he?"

"Yes. I didn't want him going into that area. I knew it would be hard on him."

"What kind of impact has it had on him now? He's a year younger than you, right?"

"Yes. But he's twenty years more cynical about marriage and relationships. And he's in love with someone but won't go near her because he's afraid it will turn out like the marriages he's hired to help end."

"I guess some of his cases become pretty bitter, don't they?"

Ryker nodded sagely. "Some of them, yes. There have been physical battles he's had to break up when the husband and wife start tearing into each other."

She cringed, picturing the problems that would create. "Why did he choose to go into that area anyway?"

"He dated a lot of girls in high school and college, several of whom weren't..." he hesitated, trying to come up with the right way to express Xander's female problems.

"Moral?" she offered, starting to see the issue. "Honest? Ethical? Are you trying to beat around the bush and tell me that he dated women who cheated on their boyfriends?"

"Not intentionally. At least not at first. Xander was the kind of guy who is charming and laughs a lot. Women are drawn to him like flies to honey. And he loves them all right back. But when he discovered that some of them had promised themselves to another guy, he was devastated that he'd broken up their relationship. He had a sort of....reputation for being..."

Cricket smiled, realizing he was trying to be honest but still keep his brother's confidences. "Good in bed?" she offered again. "Like you?"

Ryker winked at her but nodded. "My dating habits would be pathetic when compared to Xander's previous lifestyle."

She nodded, knowing that would be a hard place to be. "But your other brothers are okay, right?"

Ryker smiled. "None of us wanted Ash to get into criminal law. But he's just as stubborn. He wanted to help the underdog."

"And what happened to him?" she asked.

"He got his eyes opened. He's still an excellent criminal defense attorney but he doesn't have that doe eyed idealism he once had. He takes a lot of pro-bono cases though. Especially when he hears that someone is being beaten down by the legal system and can't afford a good attorney."

"And does that cause friction among the four of you?" she asked, already knowing the answer.

"Not at all. We all take pro bono cases. More than we're required to take but we back each other up. Especially when there's a personal issue involved."

The waiter took their dinner plates away and she felt slightly bereft, not sure what to do with her hands now. Eating the meal had acted as a sort of buffer. And Ryker had carried the conversation while trying to demonstrate that he'd also had a non-traditional upbringing. But he had no idea what he was getting into with her family. Now she fiddled with her wine glass, wondering how to completely break things off with him.

"Anyway..." she started to say. The waiter interrupted her once again with the largest, most decadent piece of chocolate cake she'd ever seen. And it wasn't just a chocolate cake. There was fudge, chocolate whip cream, more fudge and dark, chocolate cake that looked so moist it might as well have been fudge or pudding. "You didn't," she breathed, her mouth already watering just at the sight of the dessert in between the two of them.

"I did," he teased and handed her one of the forks the waiter had placed next to the plate. "You looked stressed about pretending you don't want to see me anymore. I thought this might help break through the tension."

Cricket couldn't believe how rich and amazing the dessert tasted. With her first bite, she closed her eyes as if she were in heaven. "Oh my," she sighed. "This is amazing!"

He took a bite as well, chuckling at her glazed over eyes. "I'm glad you like it."

They sat there and ate the dessert and Cricket loved every decadent, fattening moment of it. "I'm going to have to run a few extra miles tomorrow to work this off," she said as she leaned back in her chair and wiped her mouth delicately with her linen napkin.

Ryker signed the check the waiter had brought. "I'll make sure you don't have to run those extra miles," he said and took her hand, lifting her out of her chair easily.

Cricket grabbed her purse and followed, not sure what he meant by that statement. But as soon as they were in the lobby and he'd handed the valet his ticket, he took her into his arms and kissed her. This one wasn't anything like the other two they'd shared this morning. It felt more powerful, more deliberate. And she melted just like the chocolate, clinging to him as if he were the only normal part of her world.

The valet cleared his throat, standing awkwardly behind the two of them.

Ryker pulled away, a satisfied look in his eyes when he noticed that her eyes were glazed over once again, this time from his kiss and not the chocolate cake. "Let's go," he said and took her hand, handing her into his luxurious car.

They were already driving away by the time Cricket could think properly. "Where are we going?" she asked, nervous all of a sudden.

"We're heading to my place," he said and took her hand, bringing it over so that their fingers were intertwined, but the part that made her mind go blank was the way he laid their hands on his thigh. She could feel the muscles move every time he switched from the accelerator to the brake. She didn't realize she was doing it, but she stared at their hands, or at his thigh, the entire way out to his place. Since he lived relatively close by, it was a fast trip. The next thing she knew, he was pulling into a garage, and then she was in his arms. She didn't even hesitate when he lifted her out of her seat, his expert hands already dispensing with her seat belt so she could land on his lap.

The moment he touched her in private, she was out of control. She couldn't worry about her father or possible prison issues when Ryker touched her. The differences in their backgrounds faded to nothing. She'd wanted this all day long. From the first moment he'd touched her this morning, she'd been craving his touch. All those sensors that had been suppressed after her father's visit woke up fully now, more demanding than they'd ever been.

The first time they'd come together, it had been frantic and demanding. This time, there was an urgency that she couldn't slow down. In the back of her mind, there was the possibility that this might be the last time she saw him. She needed him. All of him. Now!

He tore his mouth away, looking down at her in the dim light of the garage light but she could see that he was feeling the same urgency that she was. "Get out of the car, Cricket," he ordered her.

He left her a fraction of a second after that but by the time she realized what was going on, he was already on her side of the vehicle. He reached in and lifted her out of her seat. He didn't stop there. With demanding hands that only turned her on more, he lifted her against him, and then pressed her back against the side of the car. She didn't wait around to figure out what he might do. With shaking fingers, she ripped his tie out of the way then worked on the buttons of his dress shirt. When she finally got several buttons undone, she sighed with happiness as her fingers were able to touch his heated skin. But at that same moment, he freed her breasts from her bra. Her arms were still tangled up in both her shirt and her bra, but she didn't care. His mouth was already latching onto her nipple and she screamed out with the intense heat of his mouth there combined with the cool, night air that was in the garage.

His hand reached down and pushed her skirt up, ripping her underwear off. When she felt his finger inside her, she couldn't believe how perfect it felt. "Yes!" she sighed, closing her eyes and leaning her head back once again against the top of the car. But it wasn't enough. "More," she demanded. "Please, Ryker. Don't stop," she gasped and shifted her hips, trying to move in the way that she'd learned just a few days ago that caused so much pleasure.

And then his finger was gone! She opened her eyes, almost growling with the need to have him back there, moving inside her. She heard the foil wrapper and wanted to help him, but her arms were trapped in her blouse and bra. All she could do was hold on to his waist with her legs while his hands pushed the condom onto his erection. A moment later, his large hands were back on her hips and he didn't hesitate to fill her up. Completely!

She gasped, moving against him. The urgency only intensified as he moved deeper inside her. "More," she begged of him. And he delivered. She was already splintering apart by his third or fourth stroke. It didn't take much more before he was also pounding into her with his own climax. It was so intense, so mind-blowing, that Cricket was sure she was going to pass out from pleasure.

When her breathing had finally returned to a somewhat normal pace, she opened her eyes and looked around. Her arms were still around his neck and she thought she might be strangling him. But then she felt his feather-light kisses along her shoulders and neck and smiled because he wasn't about to asphyxiate.

"Sorry," she choked out and released the stranglehold she had on his neck.

She relaxed when she heard his chuckle. "Please don't apologize for anything, Cricket. In fact," he lifted his head and kissed her gently, "I think we might be able to do that again, but better, once we're inside."

She smiled, unable to hide her happiness after that kind of release. "I don't think I want to do it any better," she countered. "I thought I'd killed you that last time."

He threw back his head and laughed, continuing to hold her in his strong arms. "Please. I'd love to be killed like that over and over again."

He pulled back and they straightened their clothing, but he took her hand and led her through his house, straight up to his bedroom. There, he undressed her slowly, kissing every part of her gently until she was writhing underneath him once again. He took her slower this time, pulling out of her almost all the way until she begged him to come back to her. Over and over again, he took her just to the edge, but wouldn't let her fall. She was almost crying with her need before he allowed her to climax in his arms. And he was right along with her. Cricket felt him come with her and thought he was the most incredible man she'd ever met in her life.

As she lay in his arms that night, feeling his fingers stroke her gently, she worked out in her mind a plan that might allow her to enjoy his company for a little while longer. It would be difficult, but if she were extremely creative and careful, maybe she could pull it off.

For the next three weeks, she snuck around in an effort to be with Ryker without her father becoming aware. She was with him every evening and all weekend when possible but she'd never spend the night, always leaving his warm, comfortable bed about ten o'clock so she could get home at what might be a reasonable hour. She knew he was exasperated with her but she couldn't shake the feeling that her father was still around and would intervene if he found out who she was with.

CHAPTER 9

By Saturday night of that week, Ryker was fed up with her nervousness and he was irritated that she insisted on sleeping alone. The only time she wasn't looking behind her or jumping when he came up on her too quietly was when she was in his bed. He also suspected that she wasn't in this relationship for the long term. He'd never been able to discuss the future because every time he'd brought it up, she'd changed the subject quickly.

But that was going to end. He wanted this woman in his life forever. Whatever was holding her back, he was going to fix it and eliminate the issue.

"Okay, what's going on?" Ryker demanded as soon as they stepped into his house after dinner that night.

Cricket turned away from the window where she'd been trying to determine if they'd been followed. At his angry outburst, she blinked and looked up at him. "What do you mean?" she asked, already worried that she'd been too obvious.

Ryker took her hand and led her deeper into the house, setting her purse to the side of the couch while he pulled her down next to him. "Cricket, we've been sneaking around the streets of Chicago for too long. Anytime I want to talk to you, I have a new phone number to call. We always meet at out of the way places first instead of just going to your place or coming here to mine. And there isn't a moment when you aren't looking behind the cab or in my rear view mirror, as if you're trying to find out if someone is following us." He paused before he continued with, "Are you in some sort of trouble?"

Cricket actually laughed at that idea. "No. I can honestly say that I have committed no crimes for which I am running from the law," she said with a smile. She scooted closer to him, feeling his heat and enjoying the way his arms automatically wrapped around her shoulders protectively.

"So why all this cloak and dagger stuff?" he asked, relaxing back against the cushions of the deep sofa. Instinctively, he knew that something was seriously wrong, something that was keeping her from committing to him completely. But for the life of him, he couldn't figure out what it was. She was jumpy and nervous and he was damn well going to fix anything that might harm her. He'd never felt protective towards any of the women he'd dated in the past. But Cricket was different. He'd known that from the first moment he'd laid eyes on her and he wasn't going to let anything happen to her.

For the moment, he relaxed though. She was in his arms and she was safe. He had a security system in his house that was state of the art. So if anyone were trying to break in, he'd know about it before they got too close.

"What's cloak and dagger about what we've been doing?" she asked, running her hand along his thigh to distract him. She knew he was becoming impatient with her, which meant she only had a little longer to be with him before he called it quits. No one could put up with her kind of behavior for long. He'd move on to a woman who didn't have her complications.

She knew it had only been a short time, but she also knew that she was head over heels in love with Ryker Thorpe. She'd known from the start that she needed to protect herself from just this sort of occurrence, but the man was just too wonderful to not fall in love with. Every moment with him she considered a gift. Something to be cherished and stored as a memory of their time together. In too short a time, he would find someone new and she'd need all the memories to keep her warm. Because she knew she'd never find anyone as wonderful, sexy, intelligent and funny as Ryker.

Ryker sighed. "The burner phones," he started off and felt her stiffen in his arms which told him he was right on target, "the meandering drives through streets where we double back to make sure someone isn't following us, the out of the way restaurants where you're less likely to be recognized…they all add up to a person who is trying to hide something." He waited a moment then said, "What are you hiding, Cricket? I can help you if you'll just trust me."

She moved over so she was sitting on his lap. "There are some things you just can't fix," she said, then bent to kiss him tenderly. It was the first time she'd ever initiated any kind of touch. Normally, he was the one who kissed her, pulled her into his arms or even just held her hand while they were walking somewhere. It startled him initially, but she knew him well enough, knew his body and how to distract him. He'd done it often enough to her lately, although she didn't think he'd done it as deliberately as she was now doing to him. She had a small pang of guilt over her actions, but then his hands came up to cup her breasts and she wasn't able to think any more than he could.

A long time later, Ryker leaned over her. "You did that on purpose, didn't you?" he asked. He might have been angry about it another time, but she just felt too good in his arms right now.

"Did what?" she asked, running her fingers over his arms, then down his chest. If it had worked once, surely it could work again.

Unfortunately, this time he wasn't playing her game. Grabbing her fingers, he rolled over so that he had her trapped underneath him, pressing his knee between her legs so she was thoroughly under his control. To further tease her, he pulled the sheet down from her chest – not allowing her to cover up. "Now that you are subdued…" he reached over to his bedside table and pulled something out of the drawer.

She knew what he normally pulled out from that drawer and she smiled in anticipation. But what he was holding definitely wasn't what she'd been expecting. "I know we've known each other for only a short time, but…" he opened the square, black box and Cricket gasped at the stunning diamond ring that was revealed. "Will you marry me?" he asked softly, watching her to try and gauge her reaction.

Her fingers shook as she reached out, barely touching the diamond ring. It was possibly the most beautiful diamond she'd ever seen in her life, and that was saying a lot due to her mother's past.

She didn't say anything for a long time, just stared, unaware that her mouth was open and there were tears forming on her lashes.

"Should I take the absence of a rejection as an acceptance?" he teased, taking the ring out of the box and sliding it down her finger. "I love you, Cricket. I know you have secrets, but I'll eventually get you to trust me enough and we'll figure them out together."

Cricket shook her head, her eyes never leaving the gorgeous diamond that was now on her finger. She couldn't believe it. He wanted to marry her?

"You can't mean this," she said, reaching out to touch the ring with her other hand. Shaking her head, she turned to face him. She could barely see him through her tears, but since he was less than a foot away, his face was only a little bit fuzzy.

"I do mean it. I want you to marry me. I want to have kids with you and grow old with you and I want to live and laugh with you."

She shook her head. "You don't know me. You don't know my family," and she cringed with those words. They were too close to the real problem. "And don't you need someone who is a bit more…" she couldn't figure out how to say it.

"I don't want anyone more anything, Cricket. I've wanted you ever since I first saw you."

"No," she denied. She grasped onto the one reason they wouldn't work that she could openly discuss. "You need a more social person. I'm not. I don't like going out and attending parties. I don't like the social whirl that you need in your business. I like staying home and being with close friends. I can barely form words when I'm around someone who intimidates me. You should know. I was like that with you the first time we met. In fact, I think I ran away."

Ryker laughed. "That you did," he confirmed. "But I thought you were cute. And yes, I have to socialize for my business, but not nearly as much as you might think. Besides, I have three other brothers who can do that for a while. We can stay home and practice making babies," he said with a lascivious grin. Then he moved his hand moved down her waist to her hip. And then lower.

A long time later, Cricket lay in his arms, listening to his deep, even breathing as he slept, his arms wrapped around her as if he couldn't release her, even in his sleep. She knew exactly how he felt, she thought, running her fingers down his arm, reveling in the rough feeling of the hair on his forearm and the muscles on his shoulder that were bulging even in his sleep.

Cricket knew she couldn't accept his proposal. She looked down at the ring on her finger, twinkling even in the darkness. It was more beautiful because it wasn't just a ring. It had meaning. It was an important message he wanted to convey to her. And because of that, it was more precious than anything she'd ever owned.

Cricket pulled on her clothes, ignoring the tears streaming down her cheeks as she looked down at the man sleeping on the bed right next to where she'd been a moment ago. This would have to be the last time she saw him. It would even be better to find a new job just so she wouldn't be tempted to spy on him while he walked from his office building to his car.

She wiped her cheeks mercilessly as she picked up her purse. She went directly to his security system and plugged in the code, then re-armed it before slipping out the door. She might be leaving him, but she also wanted him safe in his house. Not that the alarm would keep out a serious intruder, but she doubted anyone like that was lurking about at this point in the pre-dawn morning.

She didn't call a cab until she'd walked several blocks down the street, getting strange looks from several others who were driving by. This wasn't the kind of neighborhood where a person walked places. At least not unless they were wearing exercise clothes. The people of this neighborhood walked only for cardiovascular health, otherwise driving cars worth six figures to and from their destinations.

Ryker heard the door close and rolled over, sighing as he tried to figure out what was going on with Cricket. Damn her! She had him tied up in knots worrying about her safety and what she was going to do or say next.

He looked around and breathed a sigh of relief that at least she was still wearing his ring. That was something, at least. Of course, it was no guarantee that she wouldn't hand it back to him as soon as he got into the office today.

As he stared up at the ceiling, he decided then and there that it was time to be a bit more proactive about the lovely lady. He knew she wasn't a criminal, which only meant that she was running away or trying to hide from someone who was less than savory in their daily dealings with the law.

Tossing the covers aside, he decided to go ahead and get ready for the day. He was too angry to sleep any longer and his mind was already plotting to corner his lovely new fiancée and get the information he needed. He suspected she was trying to leave him, but there was no way he was going to allow that. As he showered and dressed, he formed a plan, one that would hopefully result in Mark helping him protect the little lady until he could get her down the aisle.

He also thought about calling an old friend. Mitch Hamilton ran one of the best security firms in the world. They'd been college buddies a long time ago and had kept up with each other over the years. He'd recently married a woman named Claire, he remembered. Maybe Mitch could get together for drinks and offer some advice. Ryker decided to give Mitch a call as soon as he got into the office. He could fly down this afternoon for drinks with him and be back in time to be back in bed with Cricket before she fell asleep for the night. Or even better, maybe he could wake her up!

In the meantime, Ryker knew he had a lot to get in place before the stubborn woman got to work. He'd have to tell his brothers, he supposed. That would be an irritating conversation under the circumstances. He smiled as he thought about the expressions on their faces, almost laughing at how stunned he knew they would all be.

Well, maybe not. Ash had mentioned that his work defending Mia Paulson was important. Although, last time he checked, Ash hadn't figured out how important. Ryker realized that he'd been so caught up in what was happening with Cricket, he hadn't really checked in with his brothers lately. They'd all been going separate ways.

Something occurred to him suddenly. Autumn and Xander hadn't been sniping at each other as often as normal lately. He wondered if something had finally happened between the two of them. And Axle, come to think of it, had been acting strangely yesterday. Yes, something was definitely going on.

He finished showering and grabbed a towel, wrapping one around his waist and using another to dry his hair as he walked to his closet and considered the possibility that perhaps his brother had finally ignored his irritating resistance to being with Autumn and might have done something about it.

He certainly hoped so.

CHAPTER 10

Unfortunately, Ryker's plan was foiled by a very adept woman. He'd gone into the office, only to find that Cricket wasn't there. He called her cell phone several times, left messages but she never called him back. When he called the receptionist's desk at her company, he was told that Cricket had called in sick to work.

She didn't answer her home phone, so he continued to leave messages on her cell phone and her work phone. But by the end of the day, he hadn't heard from her.

As he was driving to her house, he received a text message that just about blew his mind. "I love you. But we can't be together," was all she said. No explanation for why they couldn't be together, no final goodbye. Nothing!

Ryker read the message but continued on to her house. There was no way he was going to allow her to get away with something like that.

But when he pulled up outside of her house, it was dark. He knocked on her door, but there was no answer. It was as if she'd simply disappeared. If it weren't for that text message, he would be worried.

As it was, he drove back to his place and poured himself a tumbler of scotch, pacing back and forth in his living room and bedroom, becoming even more furious that she'd pulled this stunt. The pacing continued until nearly midnight when he fell asleep on his couch, unable to sleep in his bed without her with him. But as his eyes faded closed, his mind went over all the things he was going to do to punish her for putting him through this kind of hell.

Never, not even in the darkest part of the night, did he allow the possibility that she would get away from him. No, that wasn't even an option.

By the end of the week, he was still fuming, but he'd taken on a different tactic. He still called her each day, but only to tell her how much he loved her as well. And to explain that he wasn't giving up on their relationship. When he flew out to Barcelona Wednesday, he called her and told her he'd be gone for two days but that he loved her. When he left Barcelona and made a stop for one of his clients in London, he called her up and told her what was going on, and that he still loved her, that he was waiting for her to come tell him what the problem was.

During that whole time, Cricket sent him one more message. "I love you, but it's just impossible," was all she texted.

Ryker smiled at the message as he walked into a meeting with his London client, shaking his head at how naïve she was.

"Twelve more hours, Love" he texted right back to her, then sat down and discussed the issue that had brought him here, all the while, thinking of what he was going to do to her when he got back to Chicago.

Cricket read the words and just about broke down in tears. She'd called in sick for the past two days but when she heard that Ryker would be out of the country, she pulled herself out from under her covers, showered and forced herself to go into the office. She knew she looked horrible, with red rimmed eyes from crying, her face looked gaunt because she'd barely eaten anything more than a glass of milk or cookies for the past three days. But the idea of food made her stomach turn over.

She wanted Ryker's arms around her so badly, her body actually ached.

If only she could figure out how to protect her parents while still seeing Ryker, she would do it. But she couldn't come up with a plan, or even an explanation for what her parents do for a living, that Ryker could believe. Well, she could if she were willing to lie to him. But she simply couldn't do that. She loved him so much and she couldn't sully those feelings with a lie. So the only alternative was for her to simply break things off with him.

Josie stopped by her office Wednesday. "How are you..." she stopped midsentence when she caught sight of Cricket's pale face and sad eyes. "You're still sick, aren't you?"

Cricket took a deep breath and nodded her head. She was sick from missing Ryker and that definitely counted in her mind. She couldn't respond verbally because her throat was raw from crying.

Josie shook her head and sat down in front of Cricket's desk. "You probably shouldn't be here," she said. "Why don't you go home and rest for another few days?"

Cricket picked up a tissue and pretended to blow her nose. "I can work," she finally said, hiding her teary eyes behind the tissue until she had herself under control. She didn't want to go home because all she did was think about Ryker and how much she missed him. At least here, she could think about something other than how much she wanted to be with him.

Josie shook her head. "I don't think you should be here. But Jason's been out of town for a while so at least you don't have to deal with his wrath." She stood up and looked down at the younger woman. "If you need anything, just give me a ring, okay?"

Cricket nodded her head and pulled a stack of invoices closer, blinking rapidly to control the next bout of tears. Damn her father! He could do anything and she'd be able to be with Ryker without any concern of her father or mother being imprisoned.

She picked up her phone and thought about calling her mother. If there was ever a time when she needed her mother's shoulder to cry on, it was now. But in the end, she put the phone down again and forced herself to work through the invoices that needed to be paid. Her mother would rush out here and pat her on the back, but Cricket's father was right. There really wasn't any way that they could continue to do what they did and for her to marry Ryker. The two words were opposite. Something had to give.

But why was she always the one that had to make the adjustments, she thought angrily as she pounded the keyboard, entering data into the accounting system. She'd grown up adjusting to their lifestyle! Wasn't it about time they started adjusting to hers? Her fingers clutched at the ring dangling from the chain around her neck, feeling the beautiful diamond as if it were the most precious thing in the world to her. She even rubbed her finger where she'd been wearing it for the past three days. Her finger felt bare, naked, without the ring. She wanted so badly to put it back on her finger, but she shook her head and forced herself to focus on her work.

She had to get over Ryker, she told herself firmly. She'd have to mail his ring back to him but the thought of not having it either on her finger or close to her heart brought up a new bout of tears and she mercilessly pushed them away.

She was exhausted by the end of the day. She thought about calling in sick the following day, but since Ryker was still in Spain, she knew she should push through and get work done. But that night, sitting at home in her tiny den, she tearfully composed a letter of resignation. She'd have to quit. She accepted that now. She'd immediately start looking for a new job, but she'd leave her current position even if she didn't have another one lined up.

She had the resignation letter in her purse for the next several days, but didn't turn it in. She kept finding excuses to not submit it, feeling a strange sense of relief at the end of each day when her supervisor walked out and the opportunity to hand in her resignation was gone.

CHAPTER 11

Walking into the building the following week, Mark caught Ryker at the door to his office. "What's up?" Ryker asked, sitting down behind his desk. His mind was flipping through all the cell phone numbers Cricket had given him over the past few weeks, trying to guess which one he was going to try this time. On the flight back from Europe, his mind had changed from anger, to one of anticipation. Cricket's text messages told him loud and clear that she loved him. There was no ambiguity there. The only question was why she felt they couldn't be together. So until he heard her explanation, he wasn't going to give up. He'd come up with a plan and he was going to get through to her, solve whatever problem she thought might be hindering their relationship and get her down the aisle.

Mark smiled eagerly. "Remember that Jason Moran fellow who was getting pranked sporadically?"

Ryker smiled at the memory, immediately picturing Cricket in his mind since she worked for the ass. "Yes. I seem to recall the visit." That was another problem he was going to resolve. Cricket hated her job. He'd help her figure out what she wanted to do, other than accounting.

"Well, I went through his security and computer systems and he seemed to just keep on adding on new high tech gadgets to try and slow this person down." Mark put his laptop down on Ryker's desk. "So a few weeks ago, I added in a few new things but also went low tech as well. And here's what I caught on what's basically a nanny-cam. Those are just small video cameras that parents put into teddy bears to catch the babysitter doing something wrong," he clarified. When Ryker nodded, he pressed a button on his computer. "I put the small camera into a picture frame that was already on his desk and here's what I caught on camera. I'm not sure when this occurred since I was only monitoring the high tech stuff. I picked up the camera last night and was looking at it at home."

Ryker watched the black and white screen carefully, not really interested in catching the person but wanting to clear the issue out of his schedule so he could pass Jason off to someone else in his department. Everything was still for several seconds, but then a movement caught his eye. Something was happening in the ceiling. It was very slow, very subtle, as if the culprit were checking things out before moving anything too quickly. But once the culprit realized that everything was okay, the ceiling tile was pushed out of place and a sexy, very feminine, black-clad body appeared to lithely drop from the ceiling to the floor. Unfortunately, as soon as the figure dropped down, Ryker's gut clenched. And it just got worse the more he watched.

The person in the video was completely masked and dressed all in black, but the form-fitting clothes showed off the culprit's figure. And it was a body he knew extremely well. In fact, he had been holding that body against his only a week ago.

Mark chuckled when the figure wrapped up several pieces of the client's office furniture in wrapping paper, thinking it was a hilarious joke, but Ryker didn't find any of it very amusing. In fact, the more he watched, the angrier he became.

So his little fiancée was a cat burglar? In this instance, she hadn't stolen anything, but what about the other times?

When the woman easily lifted herself back through the ceiling, Mark shut down the video and stood up straight, a huge grin on his face. "This still doesn't give us the person, or even a face. Whoever is doing this is smart. Brilliant, actually."

Sitting back in his leather chair, Ryker considered all aspects of the issue. If Cricket were ever discovered, he could argue that she hadn't actually done any breaking and entering since she was an employee of the company. Jason had issued badges to his employees that would give them access to the building at all times of the day and night. Ryker knew he could argue that those badges gave his employees the ability to enter. Cricket just chose a less conventional method of entry. And she hadn't stolen anything of value.

Just at that moment, an image struck him of something he'd seen in her bedroom a while ago. He'd asked her about the glass vase filled with pens that she kept on the floor of her bedroom. At the time, Cricket had said she just hated to be without pens but he now suspected that those pens were stolen property of Jason's firm.

Were they of significant value? He didn't think so. And if Jason took her to court, Ryker knew he could put the issue of the stolen items in front of the jury and Jason would be laughed out of court. He suspected there wasn't a person in the country who hadn't purposely or inadvertently stolen a pen from a hotel, office or business at least once in their life. Hell, he even had a drawer filled with pens from various places despite the fact that he kept a very good writing device in his jacket pocket.

"Have you shown this to Jason yet?" Ryker asked, his mind working, the wheels spinning.

"Not yet. I was going to call him this morning." Mark picked up his laptop, feeling pretty proud of himself.

Ryker moved his hands so they were forming a pyramid, his eyes looking over the top into nothing in particular. As he thought through all the ramifications, his index fingers tapped together. "Hold off on that for a while. We might have a conflict of interest on this issue," he said. He was already picking up his phone and dialing a number. He just hoped she'd pick up when he called this time.

Mark didn't argue, already experienced enough with the Thorpe brothers that he knew there often was more to the issue than he understood. He simply nodded his head and picked up his laptop, heading out of Ryker's office.

Cricket picked up the phone without thinking about it, feeling morose after a long, horrible weekend where she'd sat on her bed, ate popcorn and watched romantic movies by herself. Her father had called five or six times, but she was too angry with him to pick up the phone. And what was worse, Ryker had stopped calling as well.

She was miserable and irritated by her job in particular and life in general. So she forgot to look at the caller ID before answering the phone this time. "Cricket Fairchild," she said with as much enthusiasm as she could muster, which wasn't very much.

Ryker's jaw clenched. "I thought you'd lost this phone?" he challenged, wishing she were here in front of him so he could see her pretty green eyes as she lied to him.

Cricket's heard jumped into her throat as she heard his deep, sexy voice. She could also picture his angry, blue eyes and had a bit of trouble breathing for several moments. "I found it," she quickly fabricated. "What's going on?" It sounded so good to hear his voice. Her fingers clenched the phone desperately.

"Besides the fact that you snuck out of my house last week before five in the morning without saying goodbye, disappeared from my life, tried to push me away and have ignored my phone calls and every voice mail for the past seven days?"

There was a slight hesitation before she said, "I..." she started to say something, then stopped, her mind drawing a blank on what she could possibly explain. The only thought that popped into her mind was how much she loved him and missed him. Not seeing him over the past week had been painful but she closed her eyes, trying to be strong. She couldn't give in to the temptation to see him again. She was in too deep already.

"Don't even try to lie to me," he said with that smooth, silky voice that forewarned her that he wasn't fooling around. "I'll get to the truth eventually. And we will be together. Don't doubt that for a moment."

Cricket sighed, rubbing her forehead as a headache slowly inched up the back of her neck. Traffic was painful today and everyone seemed to be trying to get into her lane. She wished she could just turn to the right and drive to his house, but she couldn't take any more time off of work. Besides, she had to submit her letter of resignation and start getting over Ryker. As if that were possible, she thought with dread. "Ryker, you don't understand," she replied, trying to calm him down.

He took a deep breath, trying to regain his famous control. But the idea of her not telling him something, something that seemed to have the power to scare her, infuriated him because he felt powerless to help her, protect her. And it made him even angrier that she wouldn't confide in him. "You're right. I don't understand. But you're going to explain it to me as soon as you get into the office today. No more avoiding me or ignoring my messages. We're going to talk, Cricket." He looked at his watch to see the time. "I'm guessing you'll be here in about five minutes?" he suggested, assuming she was on her normal schedule.

She heard the strange undertones in his voice and reacted to that, her stomach clenching in fear. "Yes. I'm almost there, but what's going on?" Had he discovered what her parents did for a living? Did he have some information that could hurt them in some way? She went through all she knew of their projects but she was drawing a blank since she didn't talk to her parents about their "work" any longer, not wanting to hear about it.

"Come to my office instead of going to yours," he told her firmly. "We need to talk."

Cricket hung up the phone, her mind whirling in an attempt to figure out how she was going to get through this conversation with Ryker. She realized suddenly that she'd just stopped talking to him as a way to break things off, because a formal conversation where she stood in front of him and told him she couldn't see him any longer would be too painful. She might not have even gotten the words out.

Also, not having that conversation kept up the pretense that she was still with him, that she might be able to go back to him. It was a silly dream, but she'd kept it secretly burning in her heart. Maybe that was why she'd told him that she loved him. Maybe she'd been subconsciously hoping she could figure out a way to make her relationship with her parents and her lover work out.

That had been an epic failure, she realized.

She pulled into the parking garage and sat in her car, her whole body shaking with tension.

She bit her lip and tried to stifle the sob that almost burst out of her. Looking down at her hand, she gently touched the beautiful diamond he'd given her last week. She put it on her finger when she was alone, but slipped it onto the chain around her neck whenever she was around others. She'd already determined that she had to give it back to him. She just liked the idea of being his woman for a little while, pretending that she was still his when she was alone and the darkness surrounded her, when she couldn't stop the tears any longer and there was no one to witness them anyway.

She slipped the ring up and down her finger an inch, the metal now warm from her body heat. She tried to take it off, but her fingers just couldn't do the job. It wasn't that it didn't fit and was now too tight. It was only that she wanted to keep it on her finger.

She'd wear it until she got to his office, then take it off once she was there. Just so she didn't lose it, she told herself. It was a beautiful diamond, outstanding quality and color. But more than that, it was special to her.

She stepped out of her car and was about to walk across the courtyard and into Ryker's building but a flash of something caught her eye. She looked to the left where the flash had come from, but she didn't see anything out of the ordinary. Trying to look casual, she took several steps, still trying to determine what had flashed or what was causing her instincts to flare up with concern. She'd been taught by her father always to trust her instincts and right now, her instincts were screaming for her to run.

Had someone followed her? She didn't want Ryker involved in anything her father or mother might have done so if they'd angered someone, Ryker could be in danger. And that someone might be following her in order to get to her parents. Especially since her father seemed to be hanging around her house and office too often lately. How he knew what she was doing all the time, Cricket had no idea, but it had to stop. Especially if his activities were putting Ryker in danger!

The hairs on the back of her neck were standing up in protest. Something was definitely wrong! Instead of going to his office, she adjusted her path and headed to the deli instead. She grabbed a cup of coffee, then went directly to her own building and up into her office. Generally, she never came to the deli to purchase a cup of coffee since the coffee wasn't exceptionally good and, except when Jason was on a rampage, there was always a pot of free coffee in the office kitchen. Also not very good, but it was caffeinated which is all most people needed. In this instance, however, she was using her detour as a way to scope out the courtyard. Maybe, if someone thought she was otherwise occupied, they would be less cautious. She might catch a glimpse of who or what might be causing her instincts to be going crazy in warning.

Unfortunately, she didn't see anything out of the ordinary. At this early hour, and because of the chill that had settled over the city, there weren't even any casual walkers in the courtyard. Everyone was hurrying to or from the building with a purpose.

She left the deli, her hands at least getting warmth from the coffee she had no intention of drinking, and headed into her own building, not even glancing across the courtyard to Ryker's. She didn't want anyone associating her with someone in that building if at all possible.

When she was in her office, worriedly sitting behind her desk, she called Ryker.

"Where are you?" he demanded as soon as he picked up the phone.

"Something came up," she said, standing up and peering through the blinds in her windows to see if she could spot the person who might be following her from higher up. Still nothing, she thought with frustration. "Can I meet you later?" she asked.

There was a long sigh and Cricket could imagine Ryker's strong hand running through his thick, dark hair. Just like she'd done last night. "Cricket, what's going on?" he asked, his voice softer now. "First you avoid me for a week and now I can hear in your voice that something is seriously wrong." He paused, waiting for her to tell him what was happening but when there was still silence, he said, "I promise I can help you with whatever is going on, Cricket. You agreed to be my wife," he said even more softly. "That means sharing one's problems and concerns."

Cricket closed her eyes to try and stop the tears. "I don't think…" she started to say but because he was so wonderful and she loved him so much, she just couldn't say anything more. She needed to tell him that she couldn't marry him, but that wasn't a conversation one could have over the phone. "I love you. I truly do, but I can't talk now," she said, angry that her voice broke while she spoke, revealing how deeply she was upset. "I'll call you later," she said and hung up the phone.

She sat down at her desk again, grabbing a tissue to sop up the tears and try to repair her makeup.

Taking deep, calming breaths, she refused to let her mind even think of Ryker. It took her several minutes, but she finally got the tears under control. She had to simply put him out of her mind…

The door to her office opened causing her to spin around in surprise. "What's going on?" a deep voice demanded.

Cricket looked up from her desk, her mouth falling open in astonishment as Ryker himself stood in her office looking awesome and terrifying.

It had felt like a century since she'd feasted her eyes on him and he looked…magnificent! She had no idea how long she stood there staring at him, but she felt all warm and wonderful as she drank in his tall, strong appearance.

And then the reality of his presence reached her and she jumped up. "What are you doing here?" she demanded in a whisper, her heart in her throat as she worried about someone following him. She almost tripped over her desk in her rush to get to the windows so she could close the blinds. She then hurried behind him, ignoring the confused expression on his handsome face when she closed the door as well, leaning against it and taking deep breaths, trying not to hyperventilate in her panic.

Ryker watched her carefully, looking for any clue that would tell him what was going on. "I'm here because you didn't come to me this morning."

"I told you," she said, glancing up into his eyes and then down again, unable to hold his gaze when she was lying. "Something came up."

"What?" he demanded, sliding his hands into his pockets and waiting for her answer as if he had all the time in the world.

She bit her lip and looked around, frantically searching for something to distract him. "Don't you have meetings this morning?" she asked, trying to think of some reason to get him out of her office and away from her. Until she knew if he was in danger, she didn't want him close by.

"At least you're still wearing my ring," he said grimly.

Cricket's right hand came up to cover her left hand protectively. She'd forgotten to take it off and hang it around her neck. "I…we…" she glanced down at the gorgeous ring on her finger, angry that the tears were threatening again. She had to be strong. She had to protect him! "I don't think…" she started to slip the ring off of her finger but his sharp tone stopped her.

"Don't even think about it!" he growled at her, placing both hands on hers, stopping her from removing the ring as he loomed over her. "There are obviously things that we need to work out, honesty being one of them, but you're not leaving me. We're getting married, Cricket. And you're going to tell me what's going on. But in the meantime, look at this," he said and dropped a flash drive onto her desk.

Cricket felt the muscles in her neck ease up somewhat now that she didn't have to take off the ring immediately. It would have to come off eventually, but at least she had time now to savor the feeling of being engaged. Just a few more hours, she told herself. She sat down at her desk, almost falling into her chair because her knees were about to give out on her.

Picking up the drive, she looked at him curiously. "What's this?"

He crossed his arms over his chest and stood up straight. "Watch it, Cricket," he said with that commanding, deep voice that never failed to create shivers throughout her entire body.

She looked up at him, then blindly took the flash drive and plugged it into her computer. As soon as she clicked on the only file, the image of Jason Moran's office appeared but nothing was happening. It didn't matter though. As soon as she saw that office, Cricket knew exactly what was going to happen on the screen.

Sure enough, a few seconds later, she watched her digital image as she dropped from the ceiling onto the floor, crouched and ready to spring away, just as her mother and father had taught her all those years ago.

Her face and hair were covered by the mask and there wasn't really anything that one could absolutely pinpoint as evidence of Cricket's identity. Unfortunately, when she glanced up into his ice blue eyes, she knew that he knew that the person on the screen was her.

She swallowed painfully, those neck muscles tensing up once again. She pulled her eyes away from his again and looked at the screen, cringing when she watched herself wrap up Jason's chairs, computer monitor, pictures…everything in his office. Even his pens were wrapped up with pretty, pink paper with flowers on it, a design perfect for a baby shower. Exactly what his staff thought of his latest round of temper tantrums.

There was a noise outside of her office and someone knocked on her door. Cricket's eyes snapped from the computer screen to the doorway, then up to Ryker, the panic written all over her face. She quickly clicked the "stop" button, afraid of anyone seeing her on the screen even in her disguise.

With a sigh, he leaned over and said, "What are we going to do about this, Cricket?" he asked very softly.

She swallowed and there was another knock on her door. "I…um…"

The door to her office swung open and Josie jumped back. "Oh! I'm sorry to interrupt, Cricket. It's just that…" she noticed the extremely tall man standing up and looking down at her and her voice simply trailed off as Ryker's normally terrifying presence worked it's magic.

"She'll be out in a moment," he said very smoothly, almost softly.

Josie's wide eyes just stared for a full five seconds before she realized she was supposed to respond. "Um…Yes, well, okay." And Josie slowly, carefully backed out of the office, closing the door behind her.

Cricket was pretty sure that Josie was already speeding down the hallway to talk to their friends, spreading the news that Cricket had a large, overwhelming male in her office with the door closed.

Forgetting about Josie for the moment, she swallowed as she turned back, cringing as she watched the screen. Cricket was almost finished with Jason's office. A moment later, she sprung upwards and pulled herself through the ceiling tiles, exactly how she'd entered several minutes earlier. "What are you going to do about this?" she asked, her mind frantically trying to figure out a way to resolve this without her losing her job.

"What would you like me to do about it?" he asked softly, crossing his arms over his massive chest and looking down at her.

Cricket didn't like feeling this small so she stood up from her desk and took several steps backwards. "Um…If I had my preference, I'd like you to lose that file." Her mother and father would be ashamed to know that she'd left evidence.

But even worse, she didn't know what Ryker thought about her midnight escapade. Was he angry? Of course he was angry! Why wouldn't he be angry?

Ryker watched her carefully, noting that she placed her back to a solid wall instead of a window, making herself feel more secure.

He moved closer to her. When he was less than an inch away, his arm came up to brace himself against the wall behind her and his mind filled with her feminine scent, he said, "What are you willing to do to make that happen?" he asked.

She bit her lip, wondering if he was really asking that of her. Not Ryker! Please not this! She didn't like this side of Ryker. She didn't like that he seemed to be asking her to sell herself. Her eyes narrowed and she pushed against his shoulders. "Get away from me," she growled, saddened by his suggestion.

Of course he didn't move.

Ryker breathed a huge sigh of relief when she didn't go down the most obvious path. It confirmed all of his suspicions of her. She was sweet and kind, playing a simple prank on her boss but she wasn't morally corrupt. She could have sold secrets from her boss' business to his competitors but instead, she'd turned his pictures upside down, rearranged his furniture, stole his cheap, ball point pens and wrapped his office up in ridiculous wrapping paper. She wasn't malicious. She was funny and creative.

An idea suddenly occurred to him and he wondered if she might be honest enough with him to make it work.

"Give me a dollar," he said, his eyes lighting up with the feelings he had for this woman. His woman! And he protected what was his. Damn! He loved her even more now! And now that he knew she wasn't completely lying to him, he could admit that she'd looked pretty hot in that stealth outfit. He wouldn't mind seeing her in it again. Alone. In his bedroom where he could explore all those curves underneath the thin, black material.

She was completely confused. He'd gone from trying to get her to prostitute herself to asking for money? She would have sworn the look that crossed those blue eyes was relief. But why would he be relieved? That didn't make sense. And why would he need a dollar? The man was shockingly wealthy! She'd seen his house. Every room in that place had been custom designed by some fabulous architect.

Cricket blinked, not sure why he would ask something like that of her. "Excuse me?" she asked.

"Give me a dollar," he repeated softly and with pride in his voice. "Quickly Cricket," he said to add urgency to the moment. He was aware of the other employees moving about in the hallway. The work day was starting and he knew he had to get this issue resolved fast or this could blow up around both of them.

Cricket ducked under his arm and reached for her wallet. She extracted a dollar and was about to give it to him, still confused, but she pulled back when he was about to take it from her. "Why do you need a dollar?" she asked.

"Do you trust me?" he asked. He almost laughed at the wary expression that came into her eyes.

Cricket eyed him for a long moment, about to shake her head no when she heard the word, "Yes," instead. She was so surprised by her response because she never trusted anyone. She had friends and acquaintances, but never had she allowed her personal feelings to reach the level of trust. Until him. She was literally putting her life in this man's hands. He had the power to get her fired and she didn't like that. Not one little bit.

But as she looked up at him, she realized that she really did trust him. She actually trusted him completely. She knew that he'd never do anything to hurt her, not even turn her in to her boss as the culprit for the latest office splash, which Jason didn't even known about since he'd been out of town last week.

She loved him and this new sensation of loving as well as trusting someone was completely new.

"Good," he said, hiding his relief from this surprisingly complicated woman. "Then give me the dollar," he commanded her once again.

Cricket slowly handed him the dollar, her mind frantically trying to figure out what he was going to do.

Ryker took the dollar and shoved it into his pocket. "Good. Now that you've paid me a retainer, I'm your lawyer. Will you promise me never to illegally break into anyone's business, home, building or any other type of edifice that assumes security for a person?"

Cricket had to smile at the way the man covered more than a person's home or office. "I promise," she replied with a chuckle.

His ice blue eyes told her how much he loved her and she almost melted with that realization. "Good. Now here's what's going to happen," he told her, moving closer once again. He put his hands on her hips and pulled her closer. "First of all, you will never sneak out of my bed and my home again. Is that understood?"

"I understand," she replied, not agreeing, but assuring him that she grasped the meaning of his words. Perhaps a technicality, but she wasn't guaranteeing that she might not get mad at him and want to get out of his bed. Since stealth was her training, he might perceive it as sneaking.

His eyes narrowed because he knew what she was doing. "You're never going to avoid my phone calls again, never going to ignore me for any reason. When you're mad at me or have a problem, we'll work it out together." He waited for his words to sink in before he continued, "And you're going to meet me for dinner tonight. At Antoine's and we're not going to sneak out of the building and go several blocks out of our way to find out who might be tailing you or me or both of us, agreed?"

Cricket wanted to agree to this, but she simply couldn't. "Um…could we go to maybe…?"

"No," he interrupted her resolutely. "We're going to Antoine's and you're going to listen to what I have to say. And anyone who might be trying to find us will have to make a reservation there as well."

She cringed at the idea, knowing that her father was extremely creative at getting into and out of places. "I'll be there."

"Good," he said, knowing that she hadn't agreed to the route of getting to the restaurant, only that she would arrive there and possibly eat dinner with him. He was going to understand what's going on in her life, even if it drove him crazy trying to figure it out. "I'll see you at seven then."

With that, he released her and moved away, but at the last moment, he came right back and pulled her into his arms, bent down and kissed her so completely that she was clinging to him by the time he lifted his head again. She almost whimpered when he stepped backwards and she had to hold onto the desk to keep her balance.

Just as she suspected, as soon as the door was opened, Josie, Debbie and Allyson were standing at the door, obviously trying to hear what was going on. Their mouths literally dropped open when they first saw Ryker walk through the doorway. He nodded politely to them, saying a charming, "Ladies," before he moved on down the hallway and out of her line of sight.

The three women crowded into Cricket's office, all of them demanding information in very loud, very adamant voices.

Cricket stared at the three women for a long moment, her eyes bouncing from one woman to the next as they popped one question after another at her.

After several minutes of this, she raised her hands in an attempt to halt, or just slow their barrage of questions, but she stopped when she heard a gasp from Allyson.

"What's that!" she demanded, grabbing Cricket's hand while all three women bent over to view the gorgeous, large diamond on her finger.

"Did he give this to you?" they demanded. "Is he the reason you looked so horrible last week?" "Is he the reason you've ditched us so often over the past few weeks?" "I would have chosen him over us as well!" They were saying over the top of each other, oohing and ahhing over the ring. "Who is he?"

Cricket pulled her hand away, curling her fingers up so that the ring couldn't slip off of her finger. She'd completely forgotten about the ring because of Ryker's kiss or she never would have been so forgetful.

Before she could explain anything to her friends, they heard their boss's voice down the hallway, yelling for someone to bring him one thing or another. With a sigh of irritation, the three ladies rolled their eyes and filed out of Cricket's office, ready to start the work day and get the commanded items for their boss. Obviously, her boss hadn't entered his office yet or he'd be yelling for a whole other reason.

Any other day, she'd be anticipating his wrath but not today. She had too many other issues on her mind.

Cricket sat down behind her desk and immediately pulled a stack of invoices forward. She had to input all of them, ensure that they were accurate, and then get them paid. She let her fingers fly over the keyboard and was finished with the stack in record time, ignoring Jason's bellow of outrage as he tore the wrapping paper off of his office furniture. All the while, her mind was frantically trying to come up with an answer for Ryker, an explanation that he might believe and would be as close to the truth as possible without him hating her in the end.

She didn't release any of the invoices, knowing that she wasn't focusing enough which would make her accuracy plummet, but she pulled another stack of invoices forward, needing the mindless task so the other part of her brain could work through the earlier conversation with Ryker. He didn't seem to be angry but he also didn't know the whole story. And truthfully, the video didn't reveal anything of her identity, so how could Ryker know it was her who had fallen through the ceiling?

She considered all sorts of explanations throughout the day. She even forgot about grabbing something for lunch but a sandwich arrived on her desk, delivered by the receptionist at two o'clock that afternoon. "What's this?" she asked.

Sally, the receptionist, smiled at Cricket. "It was just delivered by messenger. Which is odd because a female called about an hour ago asking if you'd gone out for lunch."

Cricket stared at the sandwich and smiled. "Thanks," she said, unable to tear her eyes away from the sweet, considerate gesture. Ryker! The man was trying to soften her up, she thought as she unwrapped the sandwich. And it was even a turkey on rye with the special mustard she liked so much! They'd only gone out for lunch once, but he'd remembered exactly what she liked.

She ate up her sandwich and then sighed with the feeling of fullness and happiness that surrounded her. She didn't even realize what she was doing until she was standing in the lobby of Ryker's law firm. "Is there any chance I could speak with Ryker Thorpe?" she asked nervously.

The receptionist smiled and picked up the phone. "Do you have an appointment?" she asked.

Cricket shook her head, biting her lip. "I don't. But just tell him Cricket is here to see him if he has a moment. It isn't important so if he's…"

The door to the lobby opened up and a very sophisticated middle aged woman stepped out. "Ms. Fairchild?" she asked, extending her hand. "I'm Joan, Mr.

Thorpe's assistant. Would you like to come this way?" she asked, holding the door open for Cricket.

Cricket had already shaken the woman's hand but her mind was still reeling from the efficiency of her sudden appearance in the lobby. She stepped towards the woman's hand, looking back at the receptionist. "How did you..."

The woman laughed softly. "No, I don't have any superpowers," she replied. "I was passing by and Diane, the receptionist typed in your name. I just received it a moment ago and was passing by the lobby. It was just good timing that you arrived at the same time."

Cricket sighed, relieved that the woman wasn't that fast and efficient. That was spooky! "Is Ryker busy? I don't want to interrupt him."

"He just stepped into a meeting, but I don't think he'll mind if I pull him out for you. In fact, I'm guessing that he would be very upset if you stopped by and I didn't let him know," she said with a smile, opening a door to Ryker's large, luxurious office. "You can wait in here. Would you like some tea or coffee?" she asked.

Cricket quickly shook her head. "No, but really, you don't need to pull him out of his meeting. I don't..." Cricket wasn't really even sure what she was going to say to him. Yesterday, she'd been desolate that she couldn't see him anymore, today she'd been caught and they hadn't resolved a single thing.

"It's no problem," Joan smiled. She was already typing on her cell phone and a moment later, the door to the conference room across the hallway opened up and Ryker stepped through the doorway. The man literally took her breath away as he approached her. She couldn't tear her eyes off of him and she didn't realize that she was smiling as he walked towards her.

"Thanks Joan," he said as he passed by her. But he closed the door a moment before he took her into his arms and kissed her.

Once again, he didn't stop until Cricket's arms were wrapped around those enormous shoulders, pressing her body against his, demonstrating her need for him to continue with his attentions.

"You came here on your own," he growled low and husky when he lifted his head finally.

"You sent me a sandwich," she replied with a growing smile and an expanding feeling that this was right. Surely there was some way to work Ryker into her life without jeopardizing her parent's freedom!

His eyes turned serious. "I suspected you would be too worried about the file and dinner tonight to remember to have some lunch. And I doubt you had any breakfast, did you?" he asked.

She smiled shyly up at him, her mind frantically trying to come to terms with the problems they were facing together. But that was for later. Right now, she just enjoyed being in his arms again. "No. You're right. And you're very sweet to have thought about me. I know you're extremely busy. Did I break up an important meeting?" she asked, not even bothering to peer around his shoulders because they were too broad.

"They can wait."

She laughed, feeling giddy with his arms around her. In fact, his touch and being in his arms felt so perfectly "right", she made a snap decision right there. She'd work it out with her mother and father. Somehow, she'd make this work. "I'll tell you everything tonight," she assured him. With that decision made, she felt a huge weight lifted from her shoulders and she reached up to kiss him. He wasn't going to let her get away with the simple peck she'd intended and bent lower, deepening the kiss. He groaned and finally lifted his head. "I'll walk you out," he said to her. "Maybe I can introduce you to one or more of your future brothers-in-law."

Cricket didn't like the sound of that, but she figured if she was going to tell him about her past and her family, she might as well at least meet his brothers.

He put a hand to the small of her back as he led her through the office. They went down an elegant staircase and into a room filled with people bustling about in some sort of hurried fashion. "That's Ash over there," he said, pointing to a man who was, shockingly, taller than Ryker.

"That's your brother?" she demanded, her eyes gawking at the huge man.

Ryker looked at Ash, then back down at Cricket's astonished gaze. "Yes. Why?"

She shook her head. "I didn't think they made them any bigger than you." She laughed when she looked up and noticed Ryker's half smile. "Are all of your brothers your size?" she asked.

"Yes. You have a lot to look forward to," he said and winked down at her.

She was just about to greet Ryker's brother when a picture in the man's hand caught her eye. "Are you having me followed?" she demanded of Ryker who was walking right behind her, a look of mild irritation on his handsome features with her question.

Ryker looked back at her sharply. "Why would you ask that?" he demanded. He looked over at the file Ash was holding and something clicked in his mind. "Do you know the man in that photograph?" he asked, taking the file folder from his youngest brother and handing it to her so she could see the pictures more clearly.

Cricket glared up at Ryker, wondering if all of her tension this morning had been for nothing. She looked back at the smiling couple in the picture that was paper-clipped to a heavy file folder, thinking about how much she'd disliked them the previous day, her irritation increasing as she lifted the photo up higher. "These two people are the heads of the charity my boss wants me to look into as a tax deduction. I was with them yesterday afternoon. Are you telling me you haven't had someone following me?"

Ash stepped in front of the blond beauty but his brother pushed him out of the way and put his arm around her protectively. Ash didn't have time to castigate his oldest brother right at the moment. He had to clarify this latest twist. "I don't know who you are…" he started to say.

Ryker interrupted him, not willing to let his youngest brother be rude to his fiancée, but also suspecting that Cricket wouldn't want their relationship broadcast just yet. Even that suspicion irritated him because he wanted to shout it out to everyone that this was his woman, partly because he wanted to claim her as his own but also so she couldn't get away from him like she had over the past week. Instead, he said, "This is Cricket Fairchild. She's one of my clients."

Cricket smothered a secret smile. "Okay, so now that we've established who I am," she said, relieved that Ryker hadn't announced their relationship to everyone, especially since they needed to talk about that video and he needed to hear everything she had to tell him tonight over dinner before he announced anything to his brothers, "would someone mind telling me why you are investigating the person that I'm investigating?"

Cricket hadn't noticed before because of all the confusion, but there were four police officers and a very nervous, very pretty brunette standing behind Ash Thorpe, all of whom were shifting forward, and they all seemed inordinately interested in the two people in the picture. The police officer stepped in at that moment, taking charge of the problem. "Ma'am, are you telling me that you were with this man yesterday afternoon?"

Cricket nodded her head, causing her blond curls to dance merrily around her stunning features and the police officer blushed slightly under her direct, green gaze. "Isn't that what I just said? It was a lunch meeting at their request," she explained. "He ordered steak and she had some sort of disgusting fish meal."

Several pairs of stunned eyes were looking back at her. "And you would be willing to testify to this?" the officer asked.

Cricket looked around, her green eyes trying to figure out why everyone was tense, as if her next words were of miraculous import. "Of course. Why? Has someone bankrupted his charity or something? They're very passionate about saving the whales off the coast of Greenland." Cricket had thought they were a bit too passionate but she'd taken their information, agreeing to pass it along to Jason.

Ash watched with increasing relief as Ash's eyes started to clear, a grin beginning to form on his features. "Cricket, this man was murdered recently," Ryker was explaining calmly.

She was surprised for a moment, but then laughed and shook her head. "No. He isn't dead. He was giving me a pitch to help him fund the next ship they are trying to acquire."

Cricket watched in amazement as the mood of the entire area changed. The tension was immediately gone and the pretty woman who had been standing behind the giant was almost bouncing in excitement. Cricket wasn't sure why, but she suspected that the police had been about to arrest her.

"You're the hero of the hour," Ryker said to her ear and led her out of the area after shaking his brother's hand. "Go for it," she heard him say to his brother, Ash, and then Ryker was nudging her out of the room. She peered back and saw the elation on everyone's face and knew she must have given them some incredible information.

"What's going on?" she asked when they were in the hallway.

"The woman behind my brother had been arrested for murdering her ex-fiancé. The supposed victim was the same man in the picture, the one who you met with yesterday over lunch. Which means that he wasn't murdered and he is alive and well, pulling another scam. So you not only saved the woman – whom I suspect is very important to my brother based on his activities recently – you also potentially saved several, possibly many, people from being scammed by the man in the picture. Hopefully, the police are going to turn their investigation away from murder to fraud."

Cricket's face was beaming with excitement. "That's incredible! Wow! I'm glad I was walking by at the right time," she added.

"Me too," Ryker replied, taking her into his arms, uncaring of the rest of the world as he bent down to kiss her in his very own lobby.

"I'll see you tonight," he said when he lifted his head. "And we're going to talk. You're going to tell me everything and we're going to get all of it straightened out."

She stepped out of his arms and tried to hide the worry. "Until tonight," she replied with a nervous nod. She might have mentally agreed to give him the information, but that still made her anxious. She'd never revealed any of her family history to anyone so this was a huge step for her.

She was in the hallway waiting for the elevator when the beautiful brunette appeared through the doors accompanied by another taller, stunning brunette. Both women were gorgeous but in different ways. The shorter one seemed friendlier but the taller one was willowy, like one of those top fashion models, but not that tall. And she didn't look mean. Nor did she look like she starved herself. She had a softness to her that was much more attractive than the anorexic skeletons that strolled down the runways with zero body fat and missing wisdom teeth so their cheekbones looked more pronounced.

She pressed the elevator button more harshly than was needed since she felt pale and washed out next to these two stunning women. Where was a plant to hide behind when one needed it?

"You're the woman who just helped me stay out of jail," the shorter woman said with a huge grin on her lovely face. "Are you okay?"

Cricket's thumb once again touched the ring on her finger, needing to feel it to make sure it was real. That he'd really given her such a significant symbol of the way he felt about her. He would most likely want it back by the time she finished dinner with him, but it was hers for now and she wasn't going to hide it on the chain around her neck.

"I'm okay," she said, wishing things were different and that her life wasn't so complicated. "Nothing a good martini can't fix," she replied with a self-deprecating smile. She thought about her father and Ryker, still not sure how to make everything work out for the men in her life that she loved. "Men are just so confusing!"

"Why don't you come with us? I don't know about the martinis," she cautioned, "but the margaritas at Durango's are perfect for anything that ails you."

Cricket considered the option. She didn't know these two women, but she could definitely use a night on the town with some women her own age. "I'm not sure I should be around humanity right now," she came back, thinking about the enormous issue weighing her down. Her lover or the father who loved her…what a monumental issue to overcome.

Mia laughed. "That's exactly where I am. I'm Mia Paulson," she said. "And we're heading out to celebrate me not being in jail for the rest of my life."

The willowy beauty stepped forward at that moment, extending her hand in a warm, friendly greeting. "I'm Autumn. I work as the office manager at The Thorpe Group so I really know how frustrating those men can be!"

Cricket smiled back, taking Mia's hand in hers and shaking it with more confidence than she felt. It had been a long time since she'd had friends her own age. She remembered Jason's furious rantings about his newly wrapped office and decided to take the afternoon off. She already had her resignation letter typed up, so why not? "That sounds like a perfect start to the weekend. I think I'll join you after all."

Fifteen minutes later, they were settled at one of the back tables of the local hangout, a pitcher of margaritas in front of them with three glasses, already filled. "To avoiding jail time and men!" Autumn said.

"Wait!" Autumn called out mid-toast. A moment later, Autumn jumped up and walked to another table where a woman was sitting all alone, looking like her martini might be the enemy. She had curly, bohemian hair that she tried to contain, but Cricket suspected that it didn't always cooperate. When Autumn and the new woman walked back to their table, Autumn immediately introduced her. "This is Kiera and she's one of the newest team members at The Thorpe Group."

Mia was almost dancing in her chair, so excited to meet the new woman to the group. "She's the one who found the information about Jeff's current fiancée buying the new BMW," she explained to Cricket with a huge grin. "If it weren't for the two of you, I would be in jail right now being charged with embezzlement as well as murder."

When all four of them were sitting down once again, Kiera with a full margarita as well, they proceeded to drink, eat salty chips and tear up the male population, laughing at their foibles and their challenges.

Cricket liked Ryker's office manager instantly. She might look like a stunning model, but she was much more friendly and down to earth. And apparently, Autumn had men problems just like the rest of them did.

Cricket laughed and joined in the conversation, enjoying herself immensely, feeling a connection with these women that she hadn't felt in a long, long time. Josie, Allyson and Debbie were wonderful, but they were at a different stage in their lives than Cricket. She couldn't connect with her office friends. Not the way she felt like she could talk to these three women.

She actually groaned when she saw Ryker move forward. When she saw three other men looking almost exactly like him, she glanced down at her margarita glass, wondering if she might have had more to drink than she thought. She looked back up to find that Ryker was standing behind her, taking her glass and downing the rest himself.

"What are you doing?" she asked, irritated that he would steal her drink.

"I'm saving you from yourself," he explained with a wink.

"Why are there so many of you?" she asked, turning to grin up at him, forgetting for the moment how nervous she was at having to explain her family to him. Well, and the fact that he was going to run for the hills as soon as he heard. She was just going to enjoy these last few minutes with him, her fuzzy mind told herself.

He lifted her out of her chair gently, almost laughing when she sagged against his side. "There's only one of me, my love. The rest are my brothers."

Her eyes widened. "Really? I might have been their sister-in-law!" she sighed, wishing things could end differently.

"You are going to be their sister-in-law," he countered, pulling her out of the bar. She didn't see him wave to his brothers but nor were his brothers paying much attention to him either. He noticed that each of them were coaxing, arguing and teasing their respective women out of their chairs as well. He and his brothers had been sitting at the bar listening to the four lovely women berate each of them in particular and men in general. He suspected that Cricket wasn't drunk, but she was feeling very relaxed.

At the door, he glanced back and realized that each of his brothers looked like they were feeling the exact same way he felt right at the moment. Possessive. Interesting, he thought, but he didn't have time to analyze that at this point. He wanted Cricket all alone and she was relaxed enough now with the tequila to hopefully tell him all her secrets. He should be a gentleman and just bring her home so she could sleep it off, but he wanted information. Once he knew what was wrong, he could more easily protect her. And he was damn well going to protect his woman! She wasn't going to run away from him either, which is what he suspected she wanted to do.

Cricket shivered as the cool, night air hit her. She was about to complain and pull away from Ryker but before she had a chance, a heavy coat was put around her shoulders. She looked up and Ryker was walking right next to her, wearing only his shirt because he'd taken off his jacket which was now around her, keeping her warm from his body heat.

She smiled up at him, automatically moving closer as his arm wrapped around her shoulders. "Everything turn out okay after we left?" she asked happily, enjoying the warmth of his coat as well as his arm around her like this.

He chuckled as he thought back to the scene in Durango's. "I think everything is going to be better than all right. Mia Paulson is probably right now in Ash's arms," he came back. He wasn't sure about Autumn and Xander. That could be explosive. But when he thought back to their interaction, they didn't appear to be at each other's throats tonight. Odd, he thought. And Axel was looking strangely confident of Kiera's status.

"That's great," she replied, sighing with relief that her new friend was out of danger and Ryker's arms were still around her. When they entered the exclusive restaurant, the hostess perked up as soon as she saw Ryker. "Your table is ready, Mr. Thorpe," she said and took two menus, leading them through the mostly-filled tables.

When they were seated, Cricket used her menu to cover her face while she looked around, feeling more than a little warm. She probably shouldn't have had that second margarita, she thought, trying to focus on the menu. She had no idea what she wanted to eat, having eaten too many salty chips. But she'd order something, just to satisfy Ryker.

Suddenly, that crazy feeling, as if something were very, very wrong came roaring back to life. She hadn't felt it at the bar, but she just knew that someone was here, someone trying to watch her. She looked around as inconspicuously as possible, trying to see if anyone were hiding behind a menu or looking in her direction.

When she didn't spy anyone watching her, she relaxed slightly and lowered her menu. Looking up, she knew she'd been caught once again. Ryker was watching her, his eyebrows raised in question.

Darn it! She definitely shouldn't have had that last drink! She carefully put the menu down beside her and took a deep breath, ready to tell him everything.

But at that moment, the waiter arrived. "Can I take your order?" he asked with a bit more force than she expected.

Cricket looked up at the cryptic waiter, surprise initially in her eyes but they widened in horror when she took in the crazy looking waiter standing beside their table. "Dad?" she gasped, letting the word slip out before she could stop it. Yep! Those were strong margaritas!

Her father's eyes narrowed and she suspected that his eyebrows would show his anger, if she could actually see his eyebrows. The man was wearing a wig that was so fuzzy that it covered his ears and his forehead. He was even wearing a mustache that, if one squinted and looked through several windows, might appear real.

"You look ridiculous, Dad," she told him brazenly She should be nervous and anxious that he was interfering once again, spying on her and driving her nuts. But she was only angry – and for all of the same reasons. The man was interfering and wouldn't leave her alone. "Take that horrible disguise off and get out of here. I'm talking to Ryker and I'll deal with you later."

She couldn't believe she'd just spoken to her father like that, but then again, neither could he. For the first time in her life, she was really irritated that his past was interfering in her future. She'd always protected the "family business" and all of the secrets that came along with their nefarious activities. But for some reason, probably her afternoon of drinking and getting to know the three women whom she admired greatly, she wasn't going to put up with it anymore. All the lies, the secrets, the illegal activities and the strange code of ethics, they were no longer hers. And she wasn't going to live with them any longer.

"Dad…" she started to say.

But he interrupted her. "Before you say another word, you need to know that your mother is in town as well and she's…"

"She can speak for herself," her mother interrupted imperiously from behind him, her elegant figure coming around the corner to stand beside the table.

Cricket had always admired her mother for her sophistication and fashion sense. Tonight was no exception. Her mother was wearing a lovely, pale blue Versace suit that hugged her figure in all the right places. Her hair was perfectly coiffed and pulled back off of her face to show off those famous cheekbones that had gotten her into more high society parties than any other thief in the world. Possibly because of the alcohol she'd imbibed, Cricket actually giggled at the enormous diamond necklace that graced her mother's neck. Which was completely fake!

With a haughty wave of her hand, Lydia Fairchild silently told one of the waiters to bring two more chairs to the table. Within moments, her directions had been completed. Ryker was already standing, taking her mother's hand.

"Ryker, this is my mother, Lydia Fairchild," Cricket explained with a sigh of resignation. "All of the best laid plans of mice and men often go astray..." she quoted Robert Burns and leaned back in her chair.

"It is a pleasure to meet you, Mr. Thorpe," her mother said with sincerity and a wide, gracious smile. "I'm assuming you are the gentleman who put that beautiful ring on my daughter's finger recently?" she asked.

"I am," Ryker responded calmly despite his dinner plans going so awry.

Cricket caught her father's eyes as they snapped towards her hand and his anger actually increased. She could feel his anger but she wasn't afraid of it any longer.

"Sit down, Mother," Cricket said. "Father, you too," she told him, ignoring his glare in her direction.

She was relieved when they both sat down, Ryker following as well. "Now that we're all here," she said and looked at her mother and father with irritation, "I want you to know that Ryker has asked me to marry him," she explained.

Lydia smiled, her eyes brightening with happiness. "I'm so glad for you dear. I was starting to worry that you wouldn't ever find the same exhilaration your father and I have shared throughout our lives." She looked over at Ryker, then back at her daughter. "I can tell that you have. And he is a good man," she confirmed, looking down at the diamond on her finger.

Cricket rolled her eyes. "Mother, Ryker is a good man because he is smart and sensitive and makes me laugh. Not because he has excellent taste in jewelry."

"It's always a good sign though, my love." Her mother winked at Ryker who only chuckled at the conversation.

Cricket turned to face her father, confronting his glare head on instead of avoiding the reason behind it. "Father, I know that you're worried about Mother, but I don't think..."

"Wait just a moment, dear," she interrupted and leaned forward. "Edward," she glared across the table at him. "How long have you known about Cricket's romance?" she asked carefully.

Cricket's eyes widened when her father actually squirmed in his chair. "Well, dear..."

"Don't you dare 'dear' me, Edward. What have you done?" She demanded angrily.

The waiter arrived at that moment, the real waiter, and was startled to find a guest sitting at the table in the restaurant's uniform. "Don't ask," Ryker stepped in for the benefit of the confused waiter. "Can you bring us a bottle of Hiedsieck Diamont Bleu, please?"

The waiter immediately bowed and stepped backwards, eager to bring the requested champagne quickly. But Ryker called him back, "And some coffee."

Cricket didn't even blush when Ryker looked at her overly flushed cheeks. She only smiled back at him, silently thanking him because she really didn't want to mix alcohols.

With the waiter gone, Ryker turned back to Cricket, silently asking her to proceed.

Cricket took a deep breath and looked back to her father. "Dad, I know that you are worried about Mom's reaction, but…"

"She's thrilled!" Lydia interrupted, speaking for herself and looking at her husband as if to say, "You're in trouble if you say another word."

Cricket stared at her mother, then at her father. "So what was all this stuff earlier about not worrying mom?" she demanded of her father.

Edward leaned forward, trying to smooth things over. "Your mother was shopping…"

"And she can still speak for herself," she interrupted again. "I'm thrilled dear. I'm very excited that you've finally found someone to love. And I wish you all the best." She leaned over and kissed Cricket's cheek, then sat back and glared at her husband once again.

Cricket watched the interplay between her mother and father, wishing both of them could understand what she was about to do. "I'm telling Ryker everything."

Her mother smiled gently. "Dear, there isn't really anything to tell."

Cricket blinked, then shook her head. "What does that mean?"

Lydia smiled gently. "Darling, we haven't had any special projects since you were about eight or nine years old."

"When we knew how much it bothered you," her father grumbled, crossing his arms over his chest despite the fact that the action looked uncomfortable in the ridiculous and ill-fitting waiter's jacket.

She couldn't believe what they were saying. They didn't steal? They didn't pick up "baubles" when they needed some excitement? They were the best in the business! "But, you trained me in all the ways." Could they really have retired so long ago?

"Honey, we taught you everything we know. That's what parents do," Lydia explained with a dramatic wave of her hands.

Cricket shook her head, stunned by this latest revelation. "No mother. Parents teach their children to read and turn in their homework on time, to avoid horrible men and not get drunk while at college."

Edward grunted. "You taught yourself all that stuff," he grumbled. "We taught you what you didn't know. We gave you a legacy."

Cricket didn't understand. "So all these years, what have you been living off of? How have you been able to afford your lifestyle?"

Edward smiled proudly and sat up straighter in his chair. "Just because we aren't in the business any longer doesn't mean we didn't invest our...profits well over the years." Edward glanced at Ryker, trying to gauge the new man's understanding of the conversation and all that it implied.

"Your father is very good at investing, dear," her mother said with pride.

She glanced between her beautiful, elegant mother and her normally handsome father, stunned. "So neither of you do...anything?"

"Well, we keep our skills up," she explained with an indignant tone. "But no, we haven't profited from our endeavors in any way. We didn't want you to feel uncomfortable any longer."

Her mind was spinning with the news that her parents hadn't stolen anything in years. Decades almost! "Why didn't you tell me?" she asked.

Both her mother and father shrugged. "We thought you knew."

Cricket fell backwards, shaking her head. "So what was all that about last week, Dad?" she demanded.

Her father sighed. "I just..."

Lydia watched her husband carefully, her heart melting for the man who had loved their daughter so deeply over the years. "He didn't want you to find a man to replace him," she said, staring pointedly at her husband. "Apologize to your daughter, Edward."

Edward shifted uncomfortably. "I didn't think you would be happy with this guy," he mumbled.

Cricket shook her head. "This is like a really bad movie!" she stated with anger rising inside of her. "Do you know what you've done to me? I was trying to protect Ryker! I thought someone was following me! But it was you all the time, wasn't it?" she asked.

The waiter arrived, startled by the rising tension from the participants at a table who, in his mind, should be celebrating. Nevertheless, he poured the sparkling wine, set the silver pot of coffee and china cup on the edge of the table, then backed away as quickly as possible, leaving the bottle in the ice bucket.

Ryker looked around the table, amazed that so much had happened in such a short period of time. "So let me get this straight, just to make sure I understand everything that has been said over the past few minutes." He looked at Edward. "You and you're wife," he glanced at Lydia, "are thieves, am I correct?" He watched them carefully, looking for signs that he was way off base.

"Retired collectors," Edward corrected firmly. "I enjoyed art collecting and my wife, she was more into the sparkly things. She collected beautiful diamonds."

Ryker's mind worked quickly. "And both of you retired as soon as you realized that Cricket didn't like the lifestyle, but you taught her all the tricks of the trade, just in case she grew up and realized that she enjoyed doing that sort of thing." Everything was clicking into place: her aversion to stealing, her midnight video where she wrapped things up, and her collection of pens in her bedroom.

"And because she had the talent for it," Edward confirmed, proud of his daughter's accomplishments.

"She's exceptionally good at it," Lydia agreed, smiling at her daughter with delight. "If only she could stomach the details." She sighed dramatically as if the details included filing papers or folding laundry versus fencing stolen articles on the black market, relieving rightful owners of their property, etcetera.

Ryker was finally getting a good picture of what was going on. "Cricket enjoys breaking into offices and pulling pranks and, up until last week, she hadn't ever gotten caught." He paused for a moment. "Am I missing anything?" he asked.

All three people shook their heads, Cricket smiling at how good he was at reading between the not-so-subtle lines. And what was even better? He didn't appear to be upset by any of what he'd heard.

Or perhaps he wasn't as calm as she thought. His next words didn't leave any room for doubt. "As Cricket's lawyer, I have to inform you that, anything you tell me is privileged information, but if I ever become aware of a crime that is about to be committed, I am required by law to inform the police."

Edward huffed and puffed a bit, irritated that someone would dare to give him orders. "So we won't talk about any of our activities with you around," Edward stated firmly as if that were the most obvious conclusion to come to.

Cricket laughed and shook her head. "That means he won't be doing anything wrong," she translated, looking directly at her father until he harrumphed and crossed his arms over his chest in a different direction.

When she'd gotten his grudging acceptance, she turned to Ryker, lifting her coffee cup in a celebratory toast. "That's all settled then," she said, her mood just as bubbly as the wine. "To the future," she said with joy.

They all raised their glass and clinked each other's, but there was something in Ryker's eyes that caused her to hesitate. She sipped her coffee, but it was hard to swallow. She was worried, wondering if perhaps he was already having second thoughts about marrying her. She had a crazy family and he didn't even know the half of it despite her father's insane disguise right at the moment.

Ryker knew exactly where her mind was going. "Don't even think it, Cricket. We're getting married. The sooner the better."

She turned to look at him more directly, wanting to understand him. That understanding probably should come before the engagement, but she hadn't done anything normal in her life so far, why start now? "So what's on your mind now?"

"That's for later tonight," he said. "Let's have some dinner."

She smiled slightly, but was still nervous about whatever he wanted to discuss with her. She picked at her meal, unable to swallow anything with her muscles clenching in fear that she was about to lose the one man who really knew how to talk to her, not to mention all the other things he did so well. She actually blushed at that thought and the man sitting across from her saw the blush. Those dark, sexy eyebrows that could silently speak so eloquently, went up in question. But when she shook her head slightly, he smiled right back at her with a wink.

Darn it! He knew exactly what she'd been thinking!

Well, she didn't really mind when it came right down to it. As long as he was going to actually act on those activities that made her blush. And just thinking of that made her whole body heat up and she looked down at her plate. She didn't want to know if he was watching her this time. It was too embarrassing how easily he could read her body language.

A few hours later, once they'd dropped her parents off at their hotel, Cricket turned slightly in her seat so she could face Ryker while he drove. He handled the powerful car expertly, not needing to weave in and out of traffic to prove his masculinity which made her much more comfortable. She was impressed with his control and his ability to be so self-assured. He wasn't cocky or arrogant but there was an aura about him that just gave one a sense of confidence.

Realizing that, she sat back and relaxed, enjoying both the ride as well as the anticipation of him taking her into his arms. At least, she hoped he was going to take her into his arms. That thought had her stiffening and looking over at him.

"What just popped into your head?" he asked as he turned down his driveway.

She considered not answering him, afraid she might sound too seductive if she said the words out loud. But then she remembered that she was trying hard to be honest with him and took a deep breath. "I was just wondering what was going to happen when we get inside your house."

He chuckled. "At this point, there shouldn't be any doubt in your mind about what is going to happen," he replied. "I've been without you for over a week. You do the math."

Her face brightened and she relaxed back against the leather seat while he drove into his garage. He didn't even wait for the garage door to close before he was out of the driver's seat and coming around the front of the car. She thought perhaps she should wait until he reached her and opened the door for her, but she couldn't wait, wanting him too desperately. After the day she'd had, she needed his touch to reassure her that they were still okay, that he hadn't changed his mind after everything he'd learned about her crazy, abnormal family.

When he reached her, he did exactly that, lifting her up into his arms and pressing her back against the car while his body pinned her there, his mouth kissing her deeply until she was trembling against him. She didn't even realize that her legs were now wrapped around his waist until he growled, "You should always wear skirts!"

"Why?" and she gasped when his teeth nibbled along her neck and shoulder.

He didn't answer. He didn't have to speak, but the way his hips pressed against hers, his arousal extremely evident, she smiled against his mouth.

She gasped when he lifted her into his arms and carried her into his house, not even pausing to turn on lights as he strode up the stairs to his bedroom. When he was finally there, he let her feet drop to the floor and he expeditiously stripped off her clothes before taking her back into his arms and kissing her silly once again. "Not fair," she gasped when her hands only encountered fabric.

"If you're not going to take advantage of a situation, then don't blame me," he teased her as he laid her in the middle of the bed. He then stood up and looked down at her, his eyes on fire as he took in her naked beauty.

She laughed but wasn't going to take that lying down. "You're a magnificent man, Ryker," she whispered.

With that, he stripped off his own clothes and took her back into his arms. With one thrust, he was inside her and she sighed with the happiness she felt as he took her higher than she ever thought possible.

CHAPTER 12

Cricket sighed as she snuggled her back up against him, enjoying his deep laughter as his large hand smoothed up her stomach, pulling her more closely against his chest. "Do that again and we'll have to start all over."

She didn't disagree with that idea, but smiled as she hugged his arm that was wrapped around her waist. "Why do you want to marry me?" she asked after a long silence. She thought that he might be asleep, but his instant response contradicted that possibility.

She could feel him smile at her question in the darkness a moment before he kissed her hair. "For the past month, each morning I would see you across the courtyard and my day would be better." His hand stroked down her hip, resting against her bottom. "And I would see you smile and everything looked more colorful. Now that I know you and feel you, I can't get enough of you. I want to spend every waking moment being with you, making you smile and protecting you."

Her smile widened and she had to close her eyes so he couldn't see the tears of happiness that welled up in them. "Is that all?" she laughed softly, but it came out as more of a hiccup than a laugh and she felt his arm come back up to hug her closely.

"Well, there's also the fact that I love you. I love your laugh and your smile. I love talking to you and laughing with you." His hand moved up to cup her breast and she gasped with the intensity of desire that streaked through her whole body. "And every time we make love, I need to do it again and again. I can't seem to get enough of your lovely, sexy body."

She turned her head, looking over her shoulder at him in the dark. "What if I get fat? Or if I get pregnant?"

He chuckled. "I'm going to work very hard at ensuring that the second one happens because I want a big family." He kissed her shoulder and said, "Only girls though, please."

Cricket giggled at his reference to his three younger brothers. "But what about my family?"

He sighed and lifted himself up onto his elbow so she was laying on her back staring up at him. "I wanted to talk to you about that until you distracted me tonight."

She laughed and playfully punched his shoulder. "I distracted you? I was innocently sitting in the passenger seat and…"

"And you got out," he stated firmly, as if all she had to do was stand up and he was ready for her.

"I don't think that actually counts as a seduction method," she argued, but her hands slid up his muscular arms, enjoying the different texture of his skin under her fingertips.

"The way you do it, it counts." And he kissed her to stop her from arguing.

Cricket was really starting to get into the kiss when he pinned her hands over her head. "We have to talk about something important though."

Her leg lifted against his thigh and she shifted slightly. "I think this is very important," she said, gasping when his hips shifted so they were right where she wanted him to be. Well…almost.

"The video file," he said and those three words were all that were needed before she was still once again, her eyes wide with fear as she looked up into his serious face.

"The file," she sighed.

"You are just like your mother and father, aren't you?"

She tried to pull away, not liking that question at all. "I'm not like them in any way," she countered, trying to pull her arms out of his but he held them gently and she wasn't able to break his hold.

"You are. You might not steal things, but I saw the look in your eyes on that video. You enjoy breaking into places, don't you?"

Cricket glared up at him, refusing to answer his question.

Ryker laughed at her attempt at being angry when she was naked under his body. "Admit it. You enjoy the adrenaline rush, don't you?"

Cricket shrugged her shoulder slightly. "Yes. Okay? I admit it! I like breaking into people's offices and houses just to see if I can. I like the thrill of not getting caught and escaping without anyone even knowing I was there. Does that mean you're out? Are you running for the hills?"

He laughed and bent lower to kiss her but when she moved her face to the side, he simply bit her ear lobe as punishment. Not hard, but enough to show her that he was still in command of her body and she shouldn't even try to hide from him.

"I think you should quit your job," he said softly, nibbling on her neck once again. "I have a friend in Virginia, just outside of Washington, D.C. who owns a security firm. I spoke to him earlier today, told him all about you. He has a division that tests companies' security systems."

She was more than a little intrigued and turned her face so she could see him in the dim light of the bedroom. "What do you mean? How does he do that?" But she knew! And her whole body was vibrating with excitement at the possibility.

Ryker laughed and shifted again, causing her to gasp. "He has a team that breaks in to buildings and figures out what the company can do better to secure their intellectual or physical property. They are a mix of ex-military and intelligence personnel, all of whom enjoy the challenge of overcoming any security system and figuring out how to make it better."

With all of her strength, she shifted and rolled on top of him. "And?" she asked, moving so she was sitting on top of him.

Ryker took her hips in both of his large hands and moved her where he wanted her to be. He loved watching her in the throes of passion. And when he filled her up, her head tilted backwards while her body adjusted to his invasion. "And..." he said as he put on a condom a moment before he shifted her hips, lifting her against him, then slowly letting her move back down, "You have an interview with him the day after tomorrow. He's interested in hiring you."

"Ryker!" she whispered with all the love and excitement she was feeling.

Those were the last words she was able to speak until she fell against his chest, her whole body draped against him as she slowly came down from her climax. "I love you," she breathed as she fell into a deep sleep, a smile on her face and her world now perfect since she was in his arms. With his job offer, she knew that he accepted all of her, quirks and craziness and everything in between.

CHAPTER 13

Cricket raced through the airport, her mind frantically trying to make a list of everything she needed to do. She was getting married in…well, soon, she thought because she wasn't really sure what day it was. But she couldn't believe her new job and even her first assignment! Mitch Hamilton had hired her during the interview, which wasn't really an interview but more of a test to challenge her skills. When she'd passed all of his tests, the man as well as several of the team members who she would be working with, stood by the "secure" building with their mouths hanging open in astonishment when she'd walked around from the back. She had to giggle at the memory of the four men, all of them huge and brawny, two with weapons strapped to their thighs cowboy style but dressed more like SWAT team members with their black cargo pants and black, knit shirts that stretched across their muscles.

All four of them were staring up at the building, waiting for her to exit from the top. So when she came around from the back, actually sneaking up on all four of them with the file folder in her hand, they swung around, prepared to do battle but froze at the sight of her smiling up at them.

The only words spoken were, "You're hired," by Mitch himself as the grins slowly evolved on the other men's faces.

The rest of the afternoon was spent going through her first assignment. She had the blueprints of the building tucked into her purse although she hadn't fully worked out how she was going to get in. Each assignment required her, or the team of personnel from Hamilton Securities, to break through a company's security system and place a note on a specific person's desk. If they were able to do that, getting in and out without anyone knowing, the mission was complete. An after-action report and security recommendations were written up and delivered to the client.

Mitch charged a crazy fee for this service but he also paid his team extremely well. He'd quoted a salary that was three times what she was earning from her accounting job. She had to give Jason Moran her notice and he was going to be furious when she wasn't able to give him the normal two week's warning. But how was a woman supposed to give two weeks notice when she had to put her house on the market, get all of her personal items moved over to her fiancée's house, plan a wedding and figure out how to break into a Fort Knox-like museum all at the same time? Something had to go and the first one was to get out of one job so she could start her new one.

Oh, and she needed to ask her new friends to be in her wedding. Yes, that would be a pretty high priority too. She sighed as she stepped out of Chicago's O'Hare Airport, about to hail a taxi to get her back to Ryker's house. She thought that maybe she could cook for him as well. Dinner…

"Need a ride, gorgeous?" a deep voice said from behind her.

Cricket dropped her arm and grinned as she spun around and threw herself into Ryker's arms. "I got the job!" she exclaimed, so excited she could barely think about anything except marrying this man and making him as happy as he made her. "I love you!" she said before standing on tip toe to kiss him.

Ryker smiled down at her, thrilled with her enthusiasm. Of course, he'd known that she'd gotten the job since Mitch had called him back earlier this morning, asking him where he'd found her. When he'd explained that Cricket was his fiancée, Mitch laughed and Ryker could even see his friend shaking his head. "You're in for a long, interesting life, my friend," he'd said.

Ryker wrapped his arm around his lovely fiancée as he walked her to his car. He certainly hoped so!

EPILOGUE

"Any chance we could announce our engagement to my brothers after the wedding?" Ryker asked, adjusting his tuxedo tie in the mirror.

Cricket had disappeared into the closet several minutes ago and he had no idea what was going on. "Cricket?" he called out, picking up the gold cufflinks Ash had given him as a groomsman gift.

Cricket emerged from the closet and Ryker's eyebrows dropped low over his eyes as he angrily looked at her figure hugging, blue satin dress. "What the hell are you wearing?" he demanded, looking at her gorgeous, lush figure wrapped up in the blue satin.

Cricket smiled warmly, spinning around for him. "I'm wearing a bridesmaid dress, silly!" She smoothed the satin down over her hips and Ryker's mouth went dry. "What do you think?"

He stared at her hard, thinking he wanted to peel that dress off of her, not take her out in it. "I think you should find something else to wear," he told her grimly.

Cricket looked up at him, surprised. She walked over to him with a huge grin on her face. "I think Mia might be trying to spur you into action," she explained as she smoothed her hands over his silk tuxedo shirt.

Ryker's hands gripped her hips firmly. "Mission accomplished," he told her as his voice became huskier while his fingers explored her curves under the satin dress. His hands stilled and he looked down at her with surprise.

"What's wrong?" she asked, nervous about the look in his eyes.

"Are all the bridesmaids wearing this dress?" he asked, thinking of one person in particular he was hoping would be wearing the same dress.

"Similar, yes," she replied, confused. "Why?"

Ryker grinned and kissed her behind her ear. "Because that means Xander is going to see Autumn in this dress."

Cricket's eyes were blank for a long moment, then she realized what he was saying and her grin matched his. "Why yes, he is!" she said and lifted up onto her toes to hug him. "Do you think it will work?" she asked, almost bouncing with anticipation and excitement.

Ryker shrugged his broad shoulders. "Nothing else has snapped those two out of their habit of fighting with each other." He'd thought they had worked out a détente recently because they'd stopped fighting but their animosity towards each other was right back, at an even higher level than before.

"I don't know why Autumn doesn't just grab Xander and kiss him," Cricket said, stepping away from Ryker to put on a pair of fake pearl earrings.

Ryker watched her, his eyebrows drawn low. "You need real pearls," he stated firmly. "And Autumn won't because Xander's been such an ass to her." He pulled a box from behind him and handed it to her.

Cricket looked at the box, afraid to touch it. "What's that?" she asked, putting her hands behind her back so she couldn't take whatever was inside.

"Why don't you open it and find out?" he suggested with an almost evil twinkle to his eyes.

Cricket shook her head. "No. It's jewelry and I'm not going to accept anything else from you. You've already spent too much with this ring," she told him, covering her engagement ring with her other hand as she often did because she loved it so much.

"Take the box, Cricket."

She shook her head. "Ryker, put it away and take it back to the store."

"Take the box," he repeated, the glint in his eyes turning into a challenge.

Cricket crossed her arms and shook her head once again. "You can't order me around," she stated firmly.

He didn't answer, but just raised one eyebrow.

She huffed. "Okay, so you can order me around in bed. Sometimes."

He chuckled and set the box down behind him. But that wasn't the end of it. He opened the box himself and pulled out a stunning diamond necklace, the icy rocks draping over his fingers like a shining waterfall.

Cricket gasped and stared hard, her whole body in shock that he would purchase something so extravagant. "No!" she whispered with reverence and indignation.

He smiled at the look and whispered back, "Yes," while kissing her neck. His hands were deft as they reached around her, fixing the clasp in place. He looked at her in their mirror, his hand smoothing out the diamonds that formed a perfect circle around her delicate neck. "That looks better," he said.

Cricket's hand went up, touching the diamonds in amazement. "This is too much," she said softly, her worried eyes catching his in the mirror. "I can't accept this."

"You don't have a choice," he replied, then reached around her and lifted the black box once again.

She almost jerked backwards when she saw the matching diamond earrings nestled in the black velvet, right in the center of where the necklace had been.

"Ryker!" she gasped but he caught her jerk against his body, his arms wrapping around her waist to hold her steady. "This is outrageous," she exclaimed.

"I now have the right to shower you with gifts," he told her, holding the earrings out in front of her. "And you'd better get used to this. I have a lot of money stored up and haven't had someone to spend it on. So deal with it. Take out the pearls, Cricket," he told her, his fingers teasing the skin on her ears.

"No. Take them back," she begged.

"I can't take them back," he laughed softly at her. "And it makes me feel good to see you in the jewels I gave you. Would you please wear them?" he asked.

When he put it that way, she couldn't really deny him. She quickly changed out her earrings and replaced them with the diamonds, then turned to face him. "You're going to spoil me," she said, grinning up into his handsome face.

"That's the plan, my love," he said and kissed her gently. "Now let's get out of here and go see how Xander deals with Autumn in that dress." He grabbed her hand and led her out the door. "Besides, the faster we get there, the sooner I can have you back here. Minus that dress."

"You're horrible," she laughed, but followed just as eagerly.

EXCERPT FROM
HIS CHALLENGING LOVER

Autumn stood by the side of the receptionist's desk, praying the woman wouldn't say the words that would once again break her heart. Unfortunately, fate wasn't playing nice today.

"I'm here to see Xander Thorpe," the blond woman with the almost dripping red lips said while flicking her thick, blond hair back over her shoulder.

Autumn knew that the hair flip was only to show off her impressive bosom, perfectly displayed by the deep V of her red dress.

Diane, the receptionist, acted professionally, exactly as Autumn had trained her. She turned to her computer with a gracious smile, her fingers poised over the keyboard as she said, "Do you have an appointment?" Diane knew that her boss, the amazingly lovely brunette with the deep, brown eyes, was standing beside her stiffly, watching to see how this exchange played out.

The blond bimbo, as Autumn now thought of her, laughed and waved her hand. "I don't, but I'm pretty sure he'll see me," she said and smoothed her hands down her hips. "Just tell him Jessica is here to speak with him."

Diane knew the process. She typed the information into the computer, then sent off the notice to Xander's assistant, currently a new woman by the name of Tilly who, at the moment was only a temporary employee, brought in yesterday when his last one quit without any notice. Xander had a bad habit of going through assistants at a horrible rate. With gritted teeth, Autumn slapped the file folder down onto the table and walked quickly out of the area. Her feet pushed her faster, desperate to not see…

She wasn't fast enough. When the woman in red entered Xander's office and closed the door, the laughter and money started exchanging hands.

"How much did you win?" James, one of the third year lawyers asked Autumn as she passed by his desk.

Autumn gritted her teeth and shook her head, walking quickly by him but trying to paste a calm-looking smile on her face. As usual, wagers were being settled now that the previous girlfriend, a lovely brunette, had been replaced by the gorgeous blond. She desperately didn't want anyone in the office to know how painful she found the betting. Xander's love life served as entertainment for the rest of the office, but it hurt her more than it should. She hated him so much! Why should she even care who he dates? He could date anyone he wanted, just so long as he kept it outside the office.

Maybe that's what bothered her so much about his philandering ways. She walked down the hallway, ignoring the jokes and the exchange of cash as bets were paid up and new ones initiated. If Xander would keep his private life more private, it wouldn't bother her so much. She preferred efficiency and order, trained her support staff to work hard, look and act professionally and be exceptionally helpful and efficient. The betting about how long the current flavor-of-the-moment would last slowed down her staff's efficiency.

Autumn knew that it happened but she never participated. Everyone thought she was just being noble and not lowering herself to petty gossip. But she knew better why she wasn't delving into the bitter world of Xander's girlfriend office pool.

Axel and Ash were walking towards her and she quickly looked down. But Axel wasn't having any of that. He caught the flash of pain in her eyes and touched her arm gently, obviously concerned.

"What's going on, Autumn? You look like you've just lost your best friend."

Autumn laughed bitterly. "Oh, goodness, nothing so dramatic as that," she came back, her shoulders squared off against the pain ripping through her. "It's just the changing of the guard." At their blank looks, she sighed and said, "Xander's old girlfriend is out and a new one is in. Everyone in the cubicles are paying up on their old bets and placing new wagers on this next woman." She was looking downwards, wishing she could just race to her own office and hide away until the pain abated, but then she caught the twenty dollar bill exchange between Axel to Ash. "That was thirty-one days, right?" he asked.

She nodded numbly, unaware that her mouth was hanging open in shock that even Xander's two younger brothers would be involved on the betting.

When those dratted tears threaten to spill over her lashes, she took a deep, frantic breath and started moving around the two extremely large men. "If you'll excuse me," she said, but didn't bother finishing the sentence as she raced down the hallway and into her office.

She wasn't aware of the two men staring after her, both of them frozen into stunned silence. "Well I'll be…" Axel said, watching until she slammed the door to her office.

Ash stopped staring at the now-closed door and grinned towards his brother. "I think that's another twenty you owe me," he said.

Axel looked at his brother, then back at the closed door one more time. "I would have sworn…" he started to say, then shook his head. "You were right." And he handed Ash another twenty. "At least it was just around us."

Ash nodded his head as well, his mouth grim with irritation over his older brother's insensitivity. "Yeah. She's usually more in control."

Axel grinned as they both turned to continue their walk down the hallway. "Want to bet on when he'll crack and admit it to her?"

Ash was already shaking his head. "Hell no! Big Brother Xander realizing what's going on?"

Both men laughed as they continued towards their destination, unaware of the woman leaning against the doorway fighting back the tears. Thankfully, Autumn didn't hear their conversation or she would have been even more humiliated. As it was, she just had to deal with the pain of seeing Xander with yet another beautiful woman. She hated this, she told herself, brutally wiping the tears from her cheeks. He was such a jerk! Why did he have to bring those women here? It was such an insult to everyone's professionalism and productivity.

He should just be more circumspect about his personal life mixing during business hours. He should never have his girlfriends trot around here like that. It was unprincipled and inappropriate!

And it hurt! Damn the man!

She sat down behind her desk and dropped her head onto her hands, trying to control the painful emotions that were threatening to choke her. She should find another job, she told herself firmly. She shouldn't put herself through the pain of watching him come and go with those women.

The idea of not being here, of not seeing…all the Thorpe brothers, caused another sharp stab of pain. She liked her job, except when there was a changing of the guard. She really shouldn't let it bother her so much. She should just look the other way and leave him to his philandering ways.

Or maybe she should talk to him, try and convince him to keep his lady-loves outside the office. Too many staff members watched them come and go. Not to mention the younger men on the staff seeing ridiculous stuff like that. Xander was a role model! He was teaching them that women were disposable, that they weren't worth the effort to invest in a real relationship.

When the meeting notification pinged, she looked at her computer and sighed. She wouldn't have time to consider that option right at the moment. She had yet another meeting to attend. Thankfully this one was just with her own staff so she wouldn't have to sit at the conference table and feel Xander's presence. Or even worse, fight the growing anger whenever he prodded her temper. The man was ingenious about getting a rise out of her and no matter how hard she tried to stay calm, she inevitably ended up firing one or two pointed jibes his way just to get back at him. He changed her, she thought resentfully. He made her act in a petty manner and she hated it. She wanted to remain calm and unemotional, to appear professional at all times. But he just kept on pushing her buttons, making her angry and forcing her temper out in the open.

She took a deep breath and grabbed a tissue out of her drawer, patting down her cheeks. With efficient movements, she pulled a mirror out of another drawer and repaired her makeup, furious that he'd reduced her to tears this time. When her face looked calm once again, she stood up and walked to the window in her office, taking several deep breaths.

Xander watched with rising fury and frustration as Autumn Hallman walked into her office, closing the door. Closing everyone out. He saw his brothers turn the corner and he made a mental note to ask them later if they knew what had upset her. He would do it now, but he had to get rid of Jessica Lilsedale. The irritating woman had attached herself to his arm last night at some charity function and he hadn't been able to get rid of her. Why had she shown up here? He'd given her absolutely no encouragement last night. And now she wanted a private word with him?

He'd gotten into the office early this morning, needing time to get work done because he had a busy schedule. Normally, the fall was a slower than normal period in his division, but not this year for some reason. Business was thriving and he was going to have to bring on a few more lawyers if this pace kept up.

He ran the family law practice in The Thorpe Group which included all family issues but mostly it came down to the divorce division. He had a thriving practice with people almost lining up at the door wanting to tear apart the spouse that, only a few years earlier, they'd promised to love, honor and cherish. It always astounded him that people who had once claimed to love each other so much that they wanted to dedicate their lives together, could reduce their entire world down to money and a desire to hurt someone as painfully as possible, in any way possible.

Jessica was rattling on and on about some inane issue. All the while, he was looking down the hallway towards Autumn's office door, willing her to come out and show her face just so he could see that she was okay. Had someone hurt her feelings? Was she overwhelmed with her work load? He'd go directly to his brothers if they were laying too much on her slender shoulders. She was just one woman but she continued to accept more and more responsibility within the firm.

Good grief, what was Jessica talking about now?

"So what do you think?" she asked, tilting her head and twirling her bleached blond hair with her talon-tipped fingers.

Xander hadn't heard a word she'd said. "I'm sorry, what was the question?"

Jessica laughed and playfully punched his shoulder. "Tonight! The party? Are you up for some fun?"

That was definitely not going to happen. With as much patience as he could muster, he walked the irritating woman to the elevators, ignoring her obnoxious chatter. "I'm sure you'll have a much better time without me," he said and took her hand, effectively releasing her grip on his arm. He lifted her hand to his lips and, as graciously as possible, kissed her fingers in an effort to send her off into the descending elevators.

As soon as she was gone, he breathed a sigh of relief. Unfortunately, the cloying cloud of perfume she left in her wake almost made him gag. Why did women insist on bathing in the rancid stuff? His mind popped to the way Autumn smelled. She was always fresh and clean. He couldn't think of a single time that she'd worn perfume. But she always smelled…incredible.

Back in the office, he stood at the end of the hallway, contemplating Autumn's closed door. She was upset and he had no idea why but it tore him apart.

He had no right to feel this way. She was an employee, and an exceptional one at that. He was one of the owners, so he should remain distant, treat her just like he would any other employee. He and his three other brothers owned equal shares in The Thorpe Group and, between the four of them, they could cover about every area of law possible.

What he couldn't cover was his need to hold Autumn Hallman in his arms. Seeing her like this, her beautiful, brown eyes filled with tears, tore him apart. He hated seeing her in pain.

What could be wrong?

She'd been with the firm for five years and she'd only become more valuable as she'd matured. And more beautiful. He'd been aching for her ever since she'd first walked through the doors looking for a job and that need had only intensified as he'd gotten to know her.

He knew that she thought of him as a royal pain in the ass. At times, he annoyed her just to see her brown eyes sparkle with anger and those pretty, pale cheeks bloom with color. And other times, he was in so much pain to possess her, to be with her and be near her that he snapped at the world. His administrative assistants bore the brunt of his irritation, but he couldn't deny the pleasure of working with Autumn every time he had to replace the previous assistant who had quit.

Of course, it helped that the last several assistants were completely inept. He wasn't one to pressure someone into quitting just so he could have one on one time with Autumn while they worked to hire a new one. No, he'd never do that to his staff. The ones that had left over the past two years had genuinely been poorly trained and ill-humored.

The last one had quit just yesterday, but he didn't mind since he'd been about to fire her anyway. The client files were a complete mess and the woman had lost track of all of his appointments, triple scheduling clients and leaving large gaps in between.

But now he felt like someone was tearing off his arm all because Autumn was upset about something. And she had to be genuinely upset because, unless she was snapping at him, she never let her emotions interrupt business. This was extremely unusual.

"Ms. Davenport is here to see you," his temporary assistant said, handing him the file.

Xander took the file with resignation. He wanted to toss the file into his office and storm down to Autumn's office so he could fix whatever had hurt her. Instead, he focused on his next client, reading through the file and skimming through the details. "She has coffee already?" Xander asked, distracted by the file and thinking about Autumn, worried that someone in the office might have hurt her feelings.

No, that was impossible. Besides him and his brothers, there wasn't anyone with as much authority in the office as Autumn. She ruled the schedules and the case loads with military precision. If anyone dared to irritate her, she quickly and efficiently put them in their place.

He loved hearing that too. When one of the other lawyers tried to get uppity, she'd simply give them a piece of her mind. Anyone who came up against the mighty Autumn Hallman went away with their tail between their legs.

Except him. He loved going head to head with her.

Unfortunately, he knew that Autumn wasn't interested in him. She had her own life, her own hobbies and plans for the future.

But he couldn't stop his eyes from looking at Autumn's closed door before he sighed and made his way into his own office. Ms. Davenport awaited. She was on her third marriage and each one made her wealthier than the last. With his help, of course.

COMMENTS FROM THE AUTHOR

For some fun visuals on Ryker and Cricket, go to:

http://www.pinterest.com/elennoxromances/his-secretive-lover-coming-dec-2013/

If you have time, please take a moment to write a review on whichever platform you purchased this book. It not only helps guide others who might purchase this book, but I also love hearing from my readers – the good, the bad and the ugly. Some readers tell me there's too much sex, some tell me I should add more, others criticize my grammar and others tell me they love my books. Everything you write, I use to improve my next story. If you love what I write, let me know because I'll continue writing in the same way. If you think I should improve in some way, please let me know. I have a very tough skin and can take it – although I absolutely LOVE the positive reviews/comments.

If you aren't already, please consider subscribing to my mailing list by signing up on www.ElizabethLennox.com. I generally only send out two emails a month: a free story introduction and a notification when a new book or free novella is available. Plus, by subscribing, you will get access to Falling for the Boss, a free novel from my Attracelli Family Series that's available only on my website!

If you would like to contact me directly, I can be reached at elizabeth@elizabethlennox.com. I try very hard to answer all e-mails because I love hearing from readers so much! It is a thrill to hear from you. But I apologize in advance if I miss responding to your message. Sometimes, things get lost in the inbox. I'm one of those non-techy people so I don't always see things that others might think are obvious. It isn't a slight – I promise. It is just that my mind is off in romance-world and not in the techy-world (much more fun/interesting/exciting in my romance-world even though my husband bangs his head against the desk sometimes when I don't understand the techy-world).

BOOKS BY ELIZABETH LENNOX

The Texas Tycoon's Temptation

The Royal Cordova Trilogy
Escaping a Royal Wedding
The Man's Outrageous Demands
Mistress to the Prince

The Attracelli Family Series
Never Dare A Tycoon
Falling For The Boss
Risky Negotiations
Proposal To Love
Love's Not Terrifying
Romantic Acquisition

The Billionaire's Terms: Prison Or Passion
The Sheik's Love Child
The Sheik's Unfinished Business
The Greek Tycoon's Lover
The Sheik's Sensuous Trap
The Greek's Baby Bargain
The Italian's Bedroom Deal
The Billionaire's Gamble
The Tycoon's Seduction Plan
The Sheik's Rebellious Mistress
The Sheik's Missing Bride
Blackmailed By The Billionaire
The Billionaire's Runaway Bride
The Billionaire's Elusive Lover
The Intimate, Intricate Rescue

The Sisterhood Trilogy
The Sheik's Virgin Lover
The Billionaire's Impulsive Lover
The Russian's Tender Lover
The Billionaire's Gentle Rescue

The Tycoon's Toddler Surprise
The Tycoon's Tender Triumph
The Sheik's Mysterious Mistress
The Duke's Willful Wife
The Sheik's Secret Twins

The Tycoon's Marriage Exchange
The Russian's Furious Fiancée
The Tycoon's Misunderstood Bride

Love By Accident Series
The Sheik's Pregnant Lover
The Sheik's Furious Bride
The Duke's Runaway Princess

The Russian's Pregnant Mistress

The Lovers Exchange Series
The Earl's Outrageous Lover
The Tycoon's Resistant Lover

The Sheik's Reluctant Lover
The Spanish Tycoon's Temptress

The Berutelli Escape
Resisting The Tycoon's Seduction
The Billionaire's Secretive Enchantress

The Big Apple Brotherhood
The Billionaire's Pregnant Lover
The Sheik's Rediscovered Lover
The Tycoon's Defiant Southern Belle

The Sheik's Dangerous Lover (free novella)

The Thorpe Brothers
His Captive Lover
His Unexpected Lover
His Secretive Lover
His Challenging Lover

The Sheik's Defiant Fiancée (Free Novella)
The Prince's Resistant Lover (Free Novella)
The Tycoon's Make-Believe Fiancée (Free Novella)

The Friendship Series
The Billionaire's Masquerade
The Russian's Dangerous Game
The Sheik's Beautiful Intruder

The Love and Danger Series – Romantic Mysteries
Intimate Desires
Intimate Caresses
Intimate Secrets
Intimate Whispers

The Alfieri Saga
The Italian's Passionate Return (Novella)
Her Gentle Capture
His Reluctant Lover
Her Unexpected Admirer (Coming November, 2014)
Her Tender Tyrant (Coming December, 2014)
His Expectant Lover (Coming January, 2015)

The Sheik's Intimate Proposition